INDEPENDENT
WITNESS

INDEPENDENT
WITNESS

Henry Cecil

ACADEMY
CHICAGO

Published in 1989 by

Academy Chicago Publishers
213 West Institute Place
Chicago, Illinois 60610

Library of Congress Cataloging-in-Publication Data

Cecil, Henry, 1902-
  Independent witness.

  I. Title.
PR6053.E3I54 1989   823'.914   88-24186
ISBN 0-89733-325-X (pbk.)

Contents

The story on which this novel is based
was first written by the author as a radio play with the
same title.

Chapter One

Hit and Run

The car stopped at the 'halt' sign and the driver looked right, left and right again. There was nothing in sight, and the car went forward, just in time to be hit broadside by a motor-cycle which had come round a sharp bend in the other road. The motor-cyclist hurtled over the top of the car and lay still. The driver stopped the car, hesitated for a moment and then drove off.

'Murder! Thieves! Stop!' shouted Colonel Brain, who was first out of the Blue Goose, the public house at the corner. 'Have you got his number?' shouted the colonel. But no one had. If anyone had expected the car to drive off, it would have been simple enough to take the number. But, as the car had stopped, none of the dozen people in the street at the time of the accident had thought it necessary. By the time they realized that they needed the number the car was vanishing out of sight. Someone said he thought the letters were CQ but that was the best they could do.

The police were on the scene within five minutes, and within ten minutes an ambulance had taken the motor-cyclist away. The police then radioed a description of the wanted car. This was not entirely easy. People were agreed that it was a sports saloon, but the colour varied. Grey, blue, and black were the most popular colours. But there was also a dark red. The common denominator was dark, and so the police called it: 'A dark sports saloon, with letters CQ and marks of a collision in the middle of the offside.'

Having dealt with the most urgent matters the senior policeman decided that there were so many witnesses and that the case was so serious that the statements would be better taken at the nearest police station, half a mile away.

They were able to give a lift to two of the bystanders but the rest, having given their names and addresses, were invited to walk. It was a dull day but not actually raining.

Colonel Brain saw old Mrs Benson on the other side of the road and went across to her. Although eighty-two she had said she preferred to walk, and so she and the colonel walked together.

'It should be prevented by law,' said the colonel. 'If that driver had been in my battalion this would never have happened.'

'Drivers!' said Mrs Benson. 'Some of them are a disgrace.'

'Do you drive, madam?' asked the colonel.

This was an awkward question for Mrs Benson. She loved driving. It was one of her dearest hobbies. But unfortunately, some three months previously, she had had an accident and been charged with dangerous driving. No one had been hurt, but the Bench considered that, if they let Mrs Benson go on driving, someone might be, and they had suspended her licence for a considerable period. A period which they thought would be sufficient to prevent her driving again in this world.

'Everyone drives today,' said Mrs Benson, 'but some of them should not be allowed to.'

'Disqualify them, I say,' said the colonel. 'That's the proper penalty. Disqualify them.'

Mrs Benson coloured slightly.

'Did you see it, colonel?' she asked.

'Did I see it?' said the colonel. 'I was first out.'

'Out?' queried Mrs Benson.

'On the scene, madam, on the scene. I saw it all. Quite disgraceful.'

'I saw it too,' said Mrs Benson. 'It was terrible.'

'There's a "halt" sign on that road,' said the colonel. 'Suppose he can't read. A foreigner, perhaps. They shouldn't be allowed to drive, madam, till they can read. A Frenchman perhaps. Do you know the French for halt, madam?'

'*Halte*, isn't it?'

8

'No, the French, madam.'

'I thought it was "*halte*". With an "e", you know.'

'But it sounds the same.'

'Yes, it does.'

'Then may I ask you, madam, what is the point of the "e"?'

'I've never thought of it like that,' said Mrs Benson.

'These foreigners!' said the colonel. 'Perhaps it was a German. D'you by any chance know the German for halt?'

'*Halt*, isn't it?' said Mrs Benson.

'But that's the same word, isn't it?' said the colonel.

'Yes.'

'Not even an "e"?'

'No.'

'Then once again, madam, I don't see the point. If it's a foreign language it should be different. That's the object of a foreign language, isn't it, to be different? But you say it's the same. Halt. Just like the English. Then how do we know he was a German?'

'You say such odd things, colonel.'

'But in English, madam, you must admit that. Anyway, the sign said "halt", and he didn't. Even without an "e" he should have understood it. But it would be a stronger case if he were German. You say it's the same in German?'

'I think so.'

'I have a feeling that he was a German, madam. Intuition, they call it. Found it very useful in my battalion. We had a corporal once who went absent without leave. He was a good chap and I felt sure it was about his wife.'

'And was it?'

The colonel thought for a moment.

'No,' he said, 'it wasn't. That was another case.'

'I see,' said Mrs Benson.

'Just an example, of course. Not on all fours. But near enough. Near enough. I hope they catch this fellow. I know what I'd have given him if he'd been in my battalion.'

'What would you have given him, colonel?'

Again the colonel was silent for a moment or so.

'As a matter of fact I couldn't have tried the case. So I

couldn't have given him anything. But if I could have given him anything I'd ... I'd ...' He stopped.

'Yes, colonel,' said Mrs Benson.

'It wouldn't make sense, madam, would it, to tell you what I would have given him if I could have given him, when I couldn't have given him.'

'I see.'

'We Army fellows haven't much brain to boast about, or so they tell us, but we try to talk sense.'

'I'm sure you do.'

'Thank you. And, if there were exams in talking sense, most of us would pass. Which is more than you can say for the Staff College. I failed twice.'

'What a shame.'

'A shame! It was a record. I'm the only person who's been allowed to fail twice. Most people are only allowed to fail once. That isn't much of a qualification. But twice, madam, that shows.'

'I'm sure it does.'

'But what does it show, madam?'

'Quite frankly, colonel, I've no idea.'

'But how could you? You weren't there. I wonder if they've caught the fellow.'

They reached the police station and were shown into a waiting room. It was some time before their turn came. Altogether there were over twenty witnesses, most of whom claimed to have seen the whole thing. As the case might result in a charge of manslaughter the police were taking no chances and they took statements from everyone. Although the details varied, sometimes considerably, they were all agreed that the car had come straight across the cross-roads without stopping and at a very fast speed. Even Colonel Brain, who had been inside the public house at the moment of impact, was quite definite on this point. And by the time he had said it often enough he really believed it.

'Now, Colonel Brain,' the officer said, 'what can you tell us?'

'I was having my morning pint when something – I can't remember what it was – made me go outside. And there was this chap tearing across the cross-roads. The poor motor-cyclist never had a chance.'

'What speed would you estimate the car was doing?'

'I couldn't be positive to a mile or two, but forty or fifty certainly.'

'At what speed did he cross the "halt" line?'

'The same.'

'And did he stop after the accident?'

'Well, he paused,' said the colonel. 'I suppose he wanted to be sure he'd killed the fellow. Apparently he was satisfied and drove on. D'you think you'll catch him, officer?'

'I expect so, sir. He must have a nasty mark on the car, and we've got the letters. If you see any cars with CQ on them will you please make a note of their numbers and let us know?'

'By Jove,' said the colonel, 'that's bright of you, officer. Why didn't I think of that?'

'We shall investigate all the CQs if necessary, but that's a long job.'

'Let's hope it *was* CQ then,' said the colonel. 'Not CG or GC or QC or QQ or CC or GG or ... but I suppose you could investigate all those too if necessary.'

'We should all be dead by then, sir. No, if it's not CQ we'll get nothing that way. But, unless he's a garage proprietor himself, the damage should help us. Of course he might lay the car up in his garage for six months or more. Then, if it isn't CQ, we've had it.'

'Don't give up, officer. I've a feeling you'll get the fellow. Intuition, you know. There was once a corporal – no, there wasn't.'

Chapter Two

Voluntary Statement

Two days after the accident Andrew Mortlake, a journalist with considerable knowledge of the Courts, called on his friend Michael Barnes, M.P. He had been asked round for a drink.

'What's wrong?' he asked, as soon as he saw Michael's face. 'Is it Sheila?'

'Yes,' said Michael.

'I'm terribly sorry. Tell me.'

'She's in hospital. The baby started to go wrong and it's been touch and go. Body and mind.'

'She's a bit better?'

'Yes. A bit. But it's terribly worrying.'

'I know. Anything I can do?'

'I'm not sure. I've got to think.'

'Well – anything at all. You know.'

'It's good of you, Andrew, but I'm not sure.'

'Not sure? I don't quite follow.'

'You couldn't,' said Michael. 'I'm trying to make up my mind whether to tell you.'

'Is it worse than you said, or what?'

'No, it's nothing to do with Sheila. Yet it is, in a way. I'm in the most frightful mess, and quite frankly I don't know what the hell to do.'

'Well, don't tell me, if you'd rather not, but it'd probably be better to get it off your chest.'

'I know, but I don't want to involve other people.'

'I can't think what you can be talking about. Is it political?'

'Only indirectly. I'd tell you if I knew more about the law. But I don't want to put you in a false position. Perhaps you know the answer. Suppose I told you I'd committed a crime, would you yourself be guilty of an offence if you didn't go to the police?'

'I've no idea. But I wouldn't go, if that's what you're afraid of.'

'That's the trouble. If I tell you – either you have to go to the police, which wouldn't suit me, or you become a criminal yourself, which wouldn't suit you.'

'But what on earth have you done? It can't be all that bad. I mean it's impossible. Have you assaulted someone in a cinema or something?'

'Oh, good Lord, no.'

'Sorry, but I can't think what it can be. You say it's not political?'

There was a pause, while the one man wondered what it was all about and the other whether to say what it was.

'I'd have read about it if you'd been had up for "drunk in charge". Anyway, you never would be.'

'No, but you're warm.'

'A motoring offence?'

'Yes. I suppose I'd better tell you. But I hope to God I'm not going to make it awkward for you.'

'Don't worry on that score. This conversation never took place.'

'Have you heard a police broadcast on the wireless asking for the driver of a car which collided with a motor-cyclist at the Blue Goose cross-roads at Needham and didn't stop?'

'I can't say that I particularly noticed it. There are so many of these police announcements. That was you?'

'Yes.'

'Why on earth didn't you stop?'

'That's the trouble. I'd just had a phone call from Sheila. She sounded terribly odd at first. Then she became hysterical and obviously dropped the receiver. I jumped into the car and raced home like hell. I came to these cross-roads and stopped. Just for a moment. I'll swear there was nothing in sight. So I went on and this wretched motor-cyclist came flying round the corner and into me. Went right over the top of the car. There were lots of people in the street. I stopped and hesitated for a moment. Well, you know how quickly the brain works. First and foremost I thought of Sheila possibly lying in a faint on the floor. The baby possibly arriving. Anything. There were lots of people to look after the poor chap on the ground. Nothing I could do for him. If I'd got out I'd have wasted at the least minutes and possibly much more. It took me half a second, I suppose, to think of all that. I made up my mind and I was off.'

'That was fair enough. I'd have done the same.'

'I got back in time to whisk Sheila off to hospital. She was sitting in a chair just looking in front of her. An awful look. She saw me and recognized me, and yet didn't seem to know me properly. I've had forty-eight hours of hell. And we're not out of it yet.'

'That's why you haven't been to the police yet?'

'That's one reason. But there's another. If they'd had my number they'd have been for me. So it looks as though they won't get me unless I go to them.'

'Aren't you going?'

'Of course I would in the normal way. But it's bound to be reported in the Press, and if Sheila sees it, it might be such a shock that she'd have a relapse. They say she must be kept absolutely quiet. Now, what the hell should I do? I really just don't know. This fellow may die. Then there'll be an inquest. I'm an M.P. It sounds dreadful not going to the police – but, if I do, it might kill Sheila – or worse. What would you do?'

Andrew thought for a moment.

'I hope to God it never happens to me. But I'll tell you what I'd do. I'd wait till Sheila's in the clear. Then I'd go to the police and explain.'

'Even if the chap died?'

'Certainly. Going to the police won't help him, or his relatives. Later on you can tell them why you did it. There's only one thing, though.'

'What's that?'

'Are you sure you can't be traced?'

'Wouldn't they have been here already if they'd got the number?'

'The whole number, yes. But, if they've only got part, they'll have a lot of weeding out to do. Might take days. Then again, you must have a mark on your car.'

'Yes, it's dented a door panel.'

'Someone might see it. If you have it put right, the garage certainly will. If you don't, it'll be there for anyone to see, and if they've got part of the number . . .'

'They have. CQ.'

'Oh Lord. That looks bad, old boy. Presumably, if they come round to you, you can't tell them lies and you'll have to admit it. Then there's only your word for it that you were going to tell them later. People aren't inclined to believe that sort of thing.'

'Then you'd go to the police now?'

'If I were sure you wouldn't be traced, I wouldn't. As I said, I'd wait until Sheila was O.K. But. if there's a chance of your being picked up, it's much too dangerous to wait.'

'Why exactly?'

'Well, I believe what you've told me about the accident. But those bystanders who saw you drive off may say anything about you. And if, in addition to that, you have to be nosed out by the police, and if the chap dies, they might charge you with manslaughter. Even if he doesn't die, they would be almost certain to charge you with dangerous driving or whatever.'

'But if Sheila sees about it in the papers?'

'You must get the staff to keep them from her. I'm sure they'll try to help. But it's much better for her to read that you were just involved in an accident than that you've got a year for manslaughter or six months for dangerous driving.'

'D'you think that's likely?'

'No, of course not, old boy, but, if the police are going to find you in the end, it'll be much worse for you if they have to come to you than if you go to them. How is the chap, by the way?'

'Well, I haven't been able to ask. But according to the papers he's still seriously ill.'

'I think you ought to go off straight away. It's much too

dangerous to risk their not tracing you. And I think they would. Unless you're a panel-beater and can repair the damage perfectly yourself they'll be round here because you're one of the CQs. Then either you show them the car or you don't. Either way, you'll have had it. And if you take it to be repaired, ten to one the garage will go to the police. No, old boy – it's not really a choice of evils. You'll have to do it. Quickly too, in case they're on the way here now. I tell you what. If you like, I'll go to the hospital and have a word with them about the papers.'

An hour later Michael was in Sandy Lane police station making a statement to a police officer. He told the officer substantially what he had told Andrew.

'You're quite sure you stopped at the "halt" line, sir?' he was asked.

'Absolutely,' said Michael. 'Not for long, though. I just looked quickly each way. There was nothing and I went on. As I told you, I was in a great hurry.'

'If I may say so,' said the officer, 'if you'll forgive me, that doesn't sound very good from your point of view. Most motorists explain that they are in no hurry at all.'

'I dare say,' said Michael, 'but I *was* in a hurry and for a very good reason. And I won't deny that I went at more than thirty in a restricted area.'

'You don't have to make any admission, sir. And, unless you want me to, I won't take down that part about the speed limit. If I may say so, sir, there may be quite enough against you without your adding any more.'

'D'you think I'm likely to be charged then?'

'It's not for me to say, sir.'

'But do you think it likely?'

'I can't say, sir, but if there are seven or eight witnesses who say you didn't stop at the "halt" line, and only one says you did, it looks . . .'

Michael interrupted him.

'I'm glad there's one person who really was looking. May I ask the name of the witness who saw me stop?'

'Well, sir, normally I wouldn't be allowed to tell you, but I can in this case. It's you, sir.'

'Oh,' said Michael, disappointed. 'And the others all say I didn't?'

'I'm not supposed to tell you that, sir. All I was going to say was that, if there are seven or eight people who said you didn't stop, I should imagine that something would be done about it.'

'Yes, so should I,' said Michael. 'When will I first hear anything?'

'You'll be notified soon enough, sir. Within a few days, I should think.'

'Thank you, officer. I'm grateful for your help.'

Michael left the police station in a very gloomy state of mind. There was bound to be a prosecution. And worse than that, he might be convicted. What would happen to Sheila? It didn't bear thinking of. He mustn't be convicted. He'd have the best counsel there was, no matter what the cost, and somehow or other he must get off. He must.

Consultation

There was a considerable sensation a week later when it was
announced that a charge was being preferred against
Michael for dangerous driving, for failing to stop at a 'halt'
line and for failing to stop after an accident. And there was
always the possibility of a charge of manslaughter being preferred. This was a certainty if the motor-cyclist did not
recover. As soon as the summonses were served on Michael,
he went to his solicitors and consulted the senior partner,
Anthony Wimbledon.

'Who's the best man in the Temple for this job?' he
asked.

'I've no doubt about that. He's a Q.C. named Olliphant.
He's not been much in the public eye, but he's first rate.
Quite young, though.'

'Shouldn't I have someone more experienced?' asked
Michael.

'There's no one really more experienced in this type of
case than Olliphant. But accident cases don't catch the
public eye, except one like yours, and he's never had to
appear for a Member of Parliament before.'

'Don't remind me,' said Michael. 'What's the great thing
about Olliphant?'

'He's brilliant with witnesses in this type of case. He's not
a particularly good lawyer, but there's no law in this. Pure
fact. And if you ask me it's one fact only. Did you stop at the
"halt" line or not? If you did, you're home. If you didn't
you're sunk.'

'What'll happen, d'you think?'

'How can I say? I must say that personally I believe what
you tell me and, if you give your evidence well, so may the

jury. Or at least they may doubt the evidence for the prosecution. But I've heard they've a tremendous number of witnesses who are going to say you didn't stop. Well, if their evidence isn't broken down, what are the jury to do?'

'I thought you said that, if I give my evidence well, the jury may believe me?'

'I did, but, if the other chaps give their evidence equally well, they may not. It's impossible to say but one thing I do know. If anyone can get you off it's Olliphant. You'll have to have a junior too, but in this case it doesn't matter who he is. Olliphant has got to do the whole case and I'll get an undertaking from him that he'll be there the whole time.'

'Like asking a surgeon not to hand over the operation in the middle to a lesser-known colleague?'

'It does sound a bit like that, I agree. But barristers are in a more difficult position than doctors. However, you needn't worry about that. If Olliphant promises to be there the whole time, he'll be there. I'll fix up a consultation with him as soon as we can. I'd like you to meet him. It might give you some confidence.'

'I need it,' said Michael. 'I've just got to get off.'

'Everything possible will be done,' said Wimbledon, 'by all of us. But ultimately it'll depend on Olliphant's handling of the witnesses. And that reminds me. It'll start before the magistrates. And, if I were you, I should have Olliphant there too. Though he probably won't ask questions or, if he does, only very few.'

'Why not?'

'He won't want to prepare the witnesses for their cross-examination in front of the jury. That's a mistake some counsel make. They try to break up the witnesses in the Magistrates' Court and in some cases may do it pretty well. But the result is that, when the fellow's cross-examined at the trial, he's ready for it all. And it's amazing how telling points can be blunted or even eliminated in this way.'

'Then why have him at the Magistrates' Court?'

'Well, it isn't essential, but, if you want to take every precaution, it'll be wise. You see, if he's there he'll have the opportunity to size up the witnesses. That's better than hearing about them second-hand. Particularly as the way a witness gives his evidence doesn't appear on the note. For example, he may hesitate a long time before saying "Yes, that is so." The pause might show he was doubtful but, unless you were there, you couldn't know it. Then again, Olliphant might ask a few questions as sighting shots. Not to give away the main attack that is coming later, but just to probe the witness's defences. To see how he responds generally to cross-examination. Whether he's the sort of man to be led gently up the garden, whether one should be stern with him or whatever.'

'Yes, I see,' said Michael. 'Well, will you engage him straight away, please. And don't mind the cost. It's not just my political career at stake, but my whole life and my wife's.'

'I understand fully,' said Wimbledon.

A few days later Michael had a consultation with Olliphant. He took Andrew with him. Wimbledon was there and their junior counsel was a quiet man called Feathers.

After Olliphant had asked Michael a few questions about his case, he said:

'Now, I suppose you're going to ask me what are your chances?'

'I am.'

'Well, I'm going to be bold in my answer. I'll say this. If you're telling me the truth, you'll get off.'

'But why should the jury believe me and not the witnesses against me? They're all independent. They've nothing against me. I don't suppose they've ever seen me or the motor-cyclist before in their lives.'

'Nothing against you?' said Olliphant. 'Haven't they? First of all, you came off best. You weren't hurt. The motor-cyclist was. When an accident happens, it's human nature to take the part of the under-dog if you haven't seen what happened.'

'But they'll say they did.'

'Of course they'll *say* they did, but the chances are they didn't. But I'll deal with that in a moment. At present I'm showing you what they've got against you. It's the old story of the big man and the little man. The car's the big man, the motor-cycle the little. It's true that some people don't like motor-cycles because of the noise they make and the way some drivers weave in and out of traffic at too high a speed. But in this case they've got a body lying on the ground badly hurt. They don't think then of exhaust noises or motor-cyclists hurtling round corners. They've got a poor mangled body in front of them. And you're quite safe in your fortress. *Of course* the tendency is to side with him. But in your case it's far worse, because you made off. If you'd stayed and explained, they might still have sided with the injured man, but some of them might have given you a hearing. But you didn't wait for one. And when you made off there can't have been one of them who didn't immediately want your blood. Anyone who makes off after an accident is naturally the object of suspicion and, at the least, serious dislike, even if no one's been hurt. But you left an injured man on the road. It's quite true that there were plenty of people to look after him, but they didn't think of that at the time. So, you see, they've a great deal against you. And it's in that frame of mind that they make their first statements. What d'you think they're going to say? None of them is going to tell deliberate lies, but they won't think they are lies. If any of them actually saw you stop at the "halt" line he isn't going to say you didn't. But the chances are that none of them really saw you at all until a split second before the crash. It's easy enough for them to think then in their prejudice against you that you didn't stop at the "halt" line. Within seconds after your departure I bet most or all of those witnesses, talking about it together before the police arrived, created a picture for themselves of you dashing across the "halt" line. By the time the police arrived, you'd charged across the line without even slowing down.'

'How on earth am I going to get off, then?'

'Well, in my opinion it all depends upon whether you are right in telling me you stopped at the "halt" line. I said before, it depends on whether you were telling me the truth. That perhaps wasn't quite correct. You might, for example, have convinced yourself that you did stop, when in fact you didn't. Remember, it was only for a moment or two anyway. What matters is not whether you believe what you've told me – as no doubt you do – but whether it's in fact correct.'

'I don't follow that,' said Michael. 'Even if it's correct – and I assure you it is – where does it get me if they all say it isn't?'

'I'll tell you. I've said that none of these witnesses are liars. However prejudiced against you, they're not going to deny something that they *know* to be true. Now, if you did actually stop, none of them can have seen that you didn't. They can imagine that you didn't, and feel quite sure now that they watched you closely and saw that you didn't. But that's because they were prejudiced against you and did not in fact see whether you stopped or not. Now, if that's the case, I believe that I can cast such doubt upon their evidence that at the least the jury won't be sure of your guilt.'

'That's very heartening, but how?' asked Michael.

'If you're telling the truth,' said Olliphant, 'it follows that what all those perfectly honest witnesses are saying is not the truth. They think it is – but it isn't.'

'How are you going to show that, with only Michael's word in his favour?' asked Andrew.

'Tell me,' said Olliphant, 'are you fond of music?'

'Music – yes, why?' said Michael, surprised.

'Can you listen to a symphony of Beethoven and read a book at the same time?' asked Olliphant.

'Well – of course,' said Michael. 'But what's that got to do with it?'

'You'll see in a moment,' said Olliphant. 'You say "of course" you can. Well, as a matter of fact, unless you happen to be a man in a million, you can't. It's physically impossible. There are a few freaks who can write two different essays at the same time, one with the left hand and one with the right hand. They're the only people who can think of two different things at the same time. And seeing requires thinking; so does listening. Take music. Naturally, while you're reading you know the music's going on – in other words there's a background of musical noise – but you can't hear the separate notes unless you stop reading. Conversely, if you listen carefully to the music you will find it quite impossible to read – that is, to take in what you're reading. You try it when you go home. You'll find I'm right, unless you cheat by stopping reading for a moment to listen to the music, and then go on reading and say you heard it all.'

'Well, I've never thought about it before. But where does it lead to?' asked Michael.

'Now I'll ask you another question,' said Olliphant. 'How often while you're awake do you think of nothing?'

'Not very often, I suppose,' replied Michael.

'Ever, d'you think?'

'I've never thought about it.'

'Well,' said Olliphant, 'you'll find with most people it's very rare indeed that they're thinking of nothing. Now another question. How long did the accident take?'

'It was all over in a flash,' replied Michael.

'Like nearly all accidents,' said Olliphant. 'Exactly. Now, immediately before this accident all those independent witnesses were in all probability thinking of something. They may have forgotten now what it was, but the chances are very strong indeed that they were thinking of something. Now, of course, some people do look at the traffic and that's what they're thinking about. But, if any honest witness was really thinking about your car just before the accident, and if you're telling the truth, he saw it stop at the "halt" line. In that case he isn't going to say it didn't.'

'Unless,' broke in Andrew, 'he's prejudiced for some reason or other – hatred of motorists for instance, or because Michael didn't stop after the accident.'

'That's true,' said Olliphant. 'But then his evidence wouldn't be honest. Prejudice is another matter which I'm going to deal with. At the moment I'm assuming all the witnesses are honest, even if prejudiced. Well, now, if none of them was *observing* your car – thinking of it – watching it – he was thinking about something else, and if he was thinking about something else he could not be thinking of your car.'

'Surely,' said Andrew, 'it might leave a photographic impression on his eye unconsciously?'

'Possibly,' said Olliphant, 'but you know yourself how dangerous photographs are. They often give a completely wrong impression. Estate agents' photographs, for example. No, it's possible but unlikely. I say that for someone consciously to notice your car, he must have stopped thinking of what he was then thinking about.'

'Unless,' said Michael, 'he was in fact looking at and thinking about my car.'

'Ah, but then he would have seen you stop,' replied Olliphant. 'In my view, if you stopped and these people honestly think you didn't, it's entirely due to prejudice. They saw you run off. There's no doubt about that, and within a few seconds they've reconstructed the accident with the scales weighted against you. And at once they say you didn't stop because they didn't, in fact, see you stop. They couldn't, because they were thinking of something else.'

'How are you going to prove that they were thinking of something else?' asked Andrew.

'By asking them questions to refresh their memory,' replied Olliphant.

'You seem very confident about it,' said Michael.

'I am,' said Olliphant, 'if, and only if, you're telling me the truth. I've seen too many independent witnesses. Most of them haven't seen the accident at all. They've heard a bang and then looked. But even if they've actually seen the collision, they only know where it happened, because they've not been following the vehicles. Of course, if they were deliberately looking at the traffic, or following the progress of some car or person, the situation is different. But then they would have seen you stop. Normally, the witness who really sees something of the accident is the person who had to be thinking about it – another driver, for instance, whose job it is to have his eyes on the road and notice some of the other traffic. That's the type of independent witness whose evidence may be of the greatest importance. But the chap who's walking along the road, thinking how he's going to pay his rent or what he's going to have for dinner – he doesn't count for much in my experience.'

'Well, that's good hearing,' said Michael. 'Because the car did stop at the "halt" sign. I know it.'

'Then,' said Olliphant, 'you'll get off.'

'That's a bold thing to say to a client,' said Wimbledon. 'I shouldn't like to.'

'Why not?' asked Olliphant. 'How many criminal cases have you personally handled where a man of whose innocence you were convinced was convicted?'

Wimbledon thought a bit.

'Well, I haven't handled a lot of criminal work, but I think I must make the answer you want. None. All the same, innocent people are convicted occasionally.'

'Very occasionally. And even more rarely in motoring cases. If you hadn't a good reason for not stopping after the accident of course the jury might be influenced against you. But you've a perfectly good explanation of that, and you came forward within a very short time. That being so, your case will be like any other accident case. The jury will think of themselves, driving your car, and be on your side from the start.'

'Where will I be tried? At London Sessions?'

'More likely the Old Bailey.'

'Why? I thought only the more important cases go there.'

'That's true. I don't want to alarm you, but, you see, if the chap dies, it'd be manslaughter, and Sessions couldn't try you for that.'

'The last report,' said Wimbledon, 'was that he was getting on fairly well.'

'Good,' said Olliphant. 'Another witness to say you didn't stop at the "halt" line. No, I don't mean that,' he added, when he saw Michael's reaction to that remark. 'I don't suppose he'll remember anything. But, if he does, you'd crossed the line by then. He could never have seen you stationary.'

'Doesn't that make it all the easier for him to say I never stopped?' asked Michael.

'Well, yes,' conceded Olliphant, 'but the distance to the point of impact from the bend from which he came is not so very much more than the distance from the "halt" line to the point of impact. He will say you were going much faster than he was and so will everyone else. So he won't be able to say that he saw you at the "halt" line at all.'

The consultation continued for a further half-hour, and then Michael and Andrew left together.

'Well,' said Michael, 'what d'you make of that?'

'Fine,' said Andrew. 'Just the man you want. He'll get you off.'

'You really believe that?'

'Convinced. You see, I believe you a hundred per cent. He says that, if you're right, you'll get off. He wouldn't be such a fool as to say that if he hadn't found by experience that he could safely make statements of that kind.'

'That may be because his clients were liars. It's easy enough if you don't believe a man to say cheerfully: "You'll get off, old boy, if you're telling the truth."'

'But I think he did believe you. Anyway, he couldn't possibly *dis*believe you at this stage. He's no grounds for doing so. No, I feel much better after that. I confess I was worried about the number of witnesses I believe they've got, but I feel better now. I think Olliphant will dispose of them. There's only one thing that could do you down,' he added. 'If you were unlucky enough to get Grampion. That would be serious.'

Chapter Four

Mr Justice Grampion

Mr Justice Grampion collected motorists. Not like a stamp collector, for pleasure, but as a duty. He believed that certainty of conviction and severity of sentence were the best inducements to motorists to drive with care. If he could choose between trying a fraud case or a charge of dangerous driving, he invariably chose the latter.

He did not drive a car himself, but it was not from envy of those who did that he became known as the terror of the motorist. Indeed, had he been a driver and personally experienced the behaviour of other drivers, his language would probably have been even stronger and his sentences more severe. So severe were they that they were even on occasions reduced by the Court of Criminal Appeal. But that did not worry him. He would pass the sentence which he considered right and, if three of his brethren chose to reduce it, that was their responsibility. He managed to resist the temptation of hoping that, on release, the motorist in question might run over each of them in turn, or at least buckle their wings.

But his sentences were not often reduced. The Appellate Court will not reduce a sentence merely because each of its members would have passed a lower sentence. The sentence appealed from must 'err in principle'. Mr Justice Grampion usually gave a man four years when another judge would have given three, or twelve months where another would have given six. It was only when he lashed out and gave ten years for what the Court thought was a three-year offence that the appellant got something knocked off.

He was as fierce in civil cases as he was in criminal, and he seldom tried an accident case in which two motorists were involved where he did not find them both to blame. And he did so in language which was carefully chosen to make each of them feel very uncomfortable indeed. It is certainly not very pleasant for a driver, who has never had an accident in twenty years' driving and who has said so in the witness-box in fairly self-satisfied tones, to hear this said about him.

'Mr Jones has told me that he has never before had an accident. I can only say that, if the evidence to which I have listened shows a fair sample of his driving, Mr Jones has been a remarkably lucky man, as indeed have those who have been within striking distance of him. His driving on this occasion, if representative of his normal driving – and, in view of his obvious satisfaction with himself, I suspect it is – if, I say, it is representative of his normal driving, it shows him to be a driver who is completely regardless of the safety, let alone the convenience of others. It is a great pity that a judge in civil cases has no power to disqualify a man from driving. I may say that, if I had such power, I should make sure that Mr Jones had no more accidents in the *next* twenty years.'

All this time Mr Smith, who was in the other car, is smiling quietly to himself. I told him he was in the wrong at the time. That'll teach him to cut corners. What wonderful language the judge uses. By Jove, I shouldn't like to be at the receiving end. Serve him damned well right. But Mr Smith does not know what is to come.

'Regarding the other driver,' the judge goes on, 'Mr – er – Mr Smith . . .'

As if to help him remember the name the judge looks round the Court and his eyes light on Smith. Smith gives a slightly nervous smile, which the next few sentences delivered by the judge swiftly remove.

'Regarding Mr Smith's driving,' repeats the judge, 'it is difficult to say whether his extraordinary manoeuvres on this occasion, which I find to be a partial cause of the accident, were due to a complete inability on his part to drive a motor car, to gross stupidity or to an utter callousness rivalling that of Mr Jones. I would certainly remove his licence, if I had the power, for the same period as I would remove that of Mr Jones. Unfortunately I have not that power, and I can only express the hope that, if either of these two gentlemen has the slightest regard for the lives or limbs or property of his fellow-citizens – which in view of the evidence I very much doubt – but if perhaps any words of mine have brought home to one of them that he is a menace on the roads, he will sell his car immediately and never drive again.'

Although only insurance companies are concerned in the ultimate result of the case, Mr Jones and Mr Smith leave the Court very red in the face. And later the same day they go red again when they read the evening papers. They disagreed with each other about everything connected with the accident, but their opinion of the judge who tried the case was identical. Indeed they might in consequence have become firm friends if they had not left the Court separately, each of them with head looking neither to the right nor left until he had got far enough away from the scene of his discomfiture not to be recognized.

Mr Justice Grampion was inclined to suggest various ways in which the motoring laws could be improved and the roads made more safe. Apart from removing licences wholesale he had suggested that it should be open to a judge who tried a motoring case to order any offending drivers to have a card fixed to the front and rear of their cars, with 'Menace' on it. Alternatively, or in addition, he suggested that a driver could be ordered to display a large red card on the top of his car facing both ways, stating the number of accidents in which he had been involved.

His summing-up to a jury in a criminal motoring case began usually something like this:

'Members of the jury,' he would say, 'today about fifteen people are going to be or have already been killed. A hundred or more have been or will be injured. When you consider your verdict in this case I would suggest that, instead of identifying yourself with the man in the dock and saying to yourselves "But for the grace of God there go I," that, instead of doing that, you identify yourself with the victims or the relatives of the victims. Consider yourself with two crushed arms and a fractured pelvis lying underneath one of these juggernauts, one of these dangerous weapons which people are allowed to brandish about as children are allowed to play with their toys. There, members of the jury, but for the grace of God lie you. And I. And all those present in Court. And before the year is up one or more of us may be one of the 6,000 done to death on the roads – and no one to shed a tear except our relatives and friends.'

And when the jury convicted and it came to sentence:

'George Robinson, your learned counsel has asked me to take into consideration that the man you knocked down in your reckless passage along the highway has recovered from his injuries and will suffer no lasting effects. No lasting effects,' he repeated, and paused. 'It is difficult to listen to such submissions temperately. But I can only say this to comfort you – and I may add that it will be the only thing that will comfort you – I am not going to increase your sentence because of the nonsense which I have been forced to listen to from your learned counsel. You may be – and indeed you are, as the facts in this case show – a callous and wicked driver, but from the way in which you gave your evidence it appears that you are not a fool. And you therefore no doubt realize, as your learned counsel apparently does not, that it is pure good luck that your victim did not die and that you do not stand in the dock facing a charge of manslaughter. For which you should know that the maximum penalty is imprisonment for life. It is not your fault that that is not the charge. We are all glad to know – even you, I expect, as well – that your victim will suffer from no lasting effects – no *lasting* effects. But he has suffered and suffered severely, and he might well have suffered death at your hands. No turn of the wheel, no application of the brake, no reduction of speed, no action or forethought, no consideration by you prevented the injuries you inflicted on this foot passenger from being fatal. But, I repeat, I am adding nothing for what almost amounts to an impertinent submission by your learned counsel. I was, however, I am afraid, raising your hopes unduly when I said that this would be of comfort to you, as, if I wanted to add anything to your sentence I could not do so, because it is plain that this offence calls for imposition of the maximum sentence, and you will go to prison for two years.'

It was small wonder, then, that motorists charged with serious offences asked anxiously who the judge was going to be, and sometimes went white when they heard.

Only one High Court judge attends the Old Bailey Sessions, and Mr Justice Grampion was often a disappointment to some members of the public who like to see the most important judge in the Court at work. He could preside at the trial of any case he chose. And usually the High Court judge was given the most important. Murder always. Manslaughter too. And even if there were no murders or manslaughters, there was usually a pleasant and varied assortment for the sightseers. Blackmail, fraud, grievous bodily harm, abduction and various sexual offences. Plenty to choose from. But what did Mr Justice Grampion do? He selected all the motoring cases. Mere dangerous driving or, at the best, motor manslaughter or causing death by dangerous driving. What a bore. What's an accident? If you're lucky you can see two or three on the way to work. The actual thing. The blood and all that. Why on earth should Mr Justice Grampion actually want to try such dull cases? The public soon learned, however, that the judge was a collector and every motorist charged with a serious offence prayed that he would not form part of the judge's collection.

Chapter Five

Colonel Brain in the Box

But the chances of a trial before Mr Justice Grampion were not great and Andrew felt fairly confident when he heard the case opened at the Magistrates' Court by Cedric Andover for the Prosecution.

'I don't propose to take up a long time in opening this case,' said Andover. 'The details will be given by the witnesses and there's no need for them to be given twice over. Suffice it to say that, at about 12.30 p.m. on the twelfth of December last, a motor-cyclist was driving along Sandy Lane towards the cross-roads by a public house called the Blue Goose. He was going at a moderate speed. He came round a bend which is only some twenty-five yards from the cross-roads. As he did so, a car came along the other road at a fast speed. It disregarded the "halt" sign in the other road and came straight across the motor-cyclist's path. A collision was inevitable. The motor-cyclist was thrown over the car and badly injured and it is wholly uncertain whether he will be available to give evidence. The car paused momentarily, then accelerated and disappeared. Later the defendant admitted that he was the driver. He said he was in a hurry to get back to a sick wife. We have no reason to doubt that statement. But it seems an insufficient reason for nearly killing a motor-cyclist. The witnesses I shall call before you are all people who were at the cross-roads at the time. They are all completely independent, and they were in a position to see the accident perfectly. None of them knew either the defendant or the man on the motor-cycle. They will all tell you quite definitely that the car came straight across the "halt" line, without stopping or even slowing down, and that that was the cause of the accident. This is a particularly dangerous cross-roads because of the bend in one of the intersecting roads. Before the "halt" sign was put up there had been a number of accidents. This is the first since it was put up. If it is correct that the accident happened in the way I have described, I submit that it is a plain and bad case of dangerous driving. It would indeed, in my submission, be a classic case of its kind. Accordingly, when you have heard the witnesses, I shall ask you to say that this is a proper case for committal. The motor-cyclist is not yet off the danger list and, though it is hoped that he will recover, in the circumstances I shall ask you to commit the prisoner to the Central Criminal Court. Call Colonel Brain.'

Colonel Brain walked smartly into the witness-box, bowed to the magistrates, looked at the clerk, hesitated and then bowed to him too. He was then duly sworn and asked his full name and address. He gave his name but asked leave to write down his address.

'Last time I gave evidence in a Court,' he explained, 'I had a number of letters. Nothing objectionable, you know, but they needed answering. And I have enough to answer without having to reply to members of the public as well.'

The chairman consulted with the clerk.

'I don't want to be difficult,' went on the colonel, 'but if even they'd enclose a stamped addressed envelope it would help. Not meanness, your Worships . . .'

'That will be all right,' said the clerk. 'The Bench will let you write down your address.'

'I'm most grateful,' said the colonel. 'I do hope you understand that it isn't meanness, it's just . . .'

'That's all right, Colonel Brain,' said the clerk. 'Would you kindly write down your address and then we can get on.'

'In block letters?' asked the colonel.

'So long as it's legible,' said the clerk.

'That's a point,' said the colonel. He thought for a moment. 'I think block would be safer.'

He wrote down his address and handed it to the clerk.

'It's not too easy to find,' he confided, 'but if you take the third on the left after . . .'

'Please, Colonel Brain, no one is going to call on you.'

'Then might I ask why you want my address?'

'The police might want to get in touch with you.'

'Without calling on me?' queried the colonel. 'I haven't written down my telephone number, I'm afraid.'

'Let's get on,' said the chairman.

'Colonel Brain,' asked Andover, 'on the 12th December last, where were you at about 12.30 p.m.?'

'I remember very plainly, sir,' said the colonel.

'Well, where was it then?'

'D'you mean at exactly 12.30 p.m., sir?' asked the colonel.

'There or thereabouts.'

'I see,' said the colonel, and paused. 'That makes it more difficult, sir.'

'Why?'

'I was in several places then.'

'You can't be in several places at the same time.'

'No, sir, but you can be in several places at *about* the same time. 12.29 is about the same as 12.30. So is 12.31. If you take a long-distance runner, sir, you would see . . .'

'I'm only concerned with *your* movements, colonel.'

'Not me,' said the colonel. 'That was my brother, H. F. Brain, the miler. He's a good example. At the beginning of a mile he'd be . . .'

'Colonel Brain, in what vicinity were you at about 12.30 p.m. on the 12th December last?'

'Vicinity?' queried the colonel. 'How big is that?'

'Were you anywhere near the Blue Goose?'

'Definitely,' said the colonel. 'The bitter's excellent.'

'Colonel Brain,' said the chairman, 'we are today concerned with an accident, not with the quality of the beer you drink.'

'Really, sir!' said the colonel, 'I have sworn to tell the whole truth.'

'Not the whole truth about your private life,' said the clerk, 'but the whole truth about an accident.'

'I don't know the whole truth about the accident,' replied the colonel. 'I know what I saw.'

'Tell us, then,' said Andover, seizing his opportunity. 'What do you remember of the accident, colonel?'

'I saw the car hit by the motor-cycle.'

'Where had the car come from?'

'I've no idea, sir. I never had the opportunity of asking him. But there's the driver, sir. You could ask him now.'

'From what direction from your point of view? Where were you standing?'

'Outside the Blue Goose.'

'Well, did it come from your right or your left or from in front of you?'

'Hadn't you better know which way I was facing, sir?' asked the colonel.

'Well, which way?'

The colonel thought for a moment.

'Upon my word, sir,' he said eventually. 'I forget. But it wouldn't really help you much. I might have turned my head.'

'Where did the motor-cycle come from?'

'From round the bend.'

'And the car?'

'It came at right angles to the motor-cycle, sir.'

'And what happened?'

'They met, sir. I don't think it was intentional.'

'When did you first see the car?'

'I saw it crossing the "halt" line, sir.'

'And did it stop at the "halt" line?'

'No, sir. I could swear to that. I said to myself...'

'No, colonel, we can't have what you said to yourself.'

'But it's part of the case, sir.'

'We still can't have it.'

'You're missing something, sir.'

'I dare say, colonel, but it's not admissible in evidence.'

'I once nearly went in for the law, but I don't remember that bit.'

'Colonel Brain,' said the chairman, 'd'you think you could confine your answers to matters which are relevant to the case?'

'I doubt it, sir,' said the colonel. 'I only started to read law. Never got very far. How do I know what's relevant? Last time I was in Court . . .'

'No, colonel, your reminiscences are most certainly not relevant.'

'Not relevant? My reminiscences? But I thought you wanted to know what I remembered of the accident? That's part of my reminiscences, sir.'

Mr Andover sat down with a sigh, and Olliphant began his cross-examination. As Wimbledon had explained, this was to be merely a gentle probing examination with no hint to the witness of what was to come at the trial – unless he was already aware of Olliphant's methods in cases of this kind.

'Colonel Brain,' he began. 'I gather you rather enjoy giving evidence?'

The colonel said nothing. After a short pause, during which Olliphant realized that, if pressed for an answer, the colonel would say he hadn't been asked a question, he added: 'Don't you?'

'The last time I gave evidence, sir,' said the colonel, 'I was nearly sent to prison.'

'For perjury?' queried Olliphant.

'No, sir,' said the colonel. 'For no reason at all that I could see.'

'How did you avoid that unpleasant consequence?'

'I have no idea, sir. It was the Lord Chief Justice, if you want to know,' he added. 'If you have to be sent to prison, I suppose it's more of a compliment to be sent by him than by anyone else.'

'But he didn't send you to prison?'

'No, sir. But it was a close thing.'

'Perhaps you talked too much, d'you think?'

'It is a family failing, sir. So it's possible. But what I was going to say, sir, is that, if one is sent to prison by the Lord Chief Justice, one can at least say "I remember once the Lord Chief Justice saying to me . . ."'

'But better if he doesn't send you to prison, surely? You can still say that, and you won't have had to go to gaol.'

'I'm obliged to you, sir. That is quite a point.'

'I suppose,' interjected Andover, 'that all this has some relevance?'

'We're coming to it – slowly,' said Olliphant. 'But, in spite of all that, you do enjoy giving evidence, don't you, colonel?'

'Enjoy?' repeated the colonel. 'I must think.'

He put his hand in his pocket and produced a small book.

'Enjoy,' he read, 'relish, like, feel pleasure, luxuriate in, revel in, riot in, swim in, wallow in ...'

'Colonel Brain,' said the chairman suddenly. 'Stop it.'

'It's a useful book, sir,' said the colonel.

'Put it away and behave yourself,' said the chairman.

The colonel took a swift glance at the book, shut it up and put it in his pocket.

'Lick one's lips,' he said. 'No, sir, I don't do that.'

'But you like it, you relish it, you revel in it, don't you?' said Olliphant.

'What a memory, sir,' said the colonel admiringly. 'Can you go on?'

'You luxuriate in it, you wallow in it.'

'Not wallow, sir. Pigs wallow. I don't care for that expression. You left out riot in it, sir.'

'Thank you, colonel,' said Olliphant. 'How would you describe your feelings in the witness-box, colonel? Like, revel, relish, which is it?'

'I enjoy it, sir,' said the colonel.

'Why?'

'Someone to talk to, sir, particularly someone I'm not likely to meet otherwise. The Lord Chief Justice, for example. Or you, sir, if I may say so. I'm hardly likely to meet either of you in the Blue Goose.'

'So you treat the witness-box as an excuse for a chat?'

'Not as an excuse, sir. I came here to tell the truth, sir. The chat is a perquisite, sir.'

'So I suppose you would take any chance you could to give evidence?'

'Not *any* chance, sir. But I'd walk across the road.'

'As you did here, colonel. I hope you've considered it worth it.'

'This is only the *hors d'œuvres*, sir, if I may say so. The real *conversazione* will take place later, will it not?'

'And,' said the chairman, 'if you behave at the Assizes as you have behaved here, you may not avoid being sent to prison this time. We have no power to commit you or we should certainly have done so. Courts of Law are very serious places. The accused here is charged with a very serious offence. A man was gravely injured. And you treat the whole proceedings with contempt. I'm also bound to add that you are aided and abetted to some extent by learned counsel for the accused. You may not know any better, though you should, Colonel Brain, but counsel does know better. And the Bench expects an apology. You both might have been appearing on some farcical radio or television show. The result of the accident might have been that a man died. The result of this case could be that a man will go to prison for years. You should both be ashamed of yourselves.'

'I'm not concerned with your criticism of Colonel Brain, sir,' said Olliphant, 'but you are not entitled to criticize me as you have. Counsel is perfectly entitled to humour an opposing witness, and that is all I have done. If neither you nor the learned clerk, nor my learned opponent, can control a witness, it is not right that you should vent your indignation at the Court's own impotence upon counsel for the accused, who has no duty to control the witness. If any apologies are due between me and you, sir, they are due from you.'

'Suppose,' said Colonel Brain pleasantly, 'suppose we apologize all round? I'm a man who never minds apologizing, even when I'm in the wrong.'

'We shall rise now,' said the chairman. 'During the adjournment I shall consult the learned clerk to see whether it is desirable that proceedings for contempt should be taken against Colonel Brain in a higher court. Some people who are aware that we ourselves have no power to commit to prison for contempt of Court are unaware that it is open to the High Court to commit someone to prison for contempt of our Court. Such proceedings might be lengthy and expensive. If Colonel Brain chooses to make a full and proper apology for his buffoonery upon the adjourned hearing it might be possible to avoid taking the course I have suggested.'

And the hearing was adjourned. On the adjourned hearing the colonel said he was sorry, though, he added, that he was unaware what for and neither Olliphant nor Andover asked him any further questions.

Chapter Six

Mr Salter

The second witness was a retired schoolmaster, Charles Salter. He gave his evidence slowly and clearly and definitely.

'I was about to go into a shop to buy some cigarettes,' he said, 'when my attention was called to a car coming fast from the other side of the cross-roads. It came on without stopping at the "halt" line. Suddenly a motor-cycle appeared and struck it broadside on. This was in the middle of the crossing. The motor-cyclist had no chance to avoid the accident.'

'He might have had a chance if he'd been going slower, mightn't he?' asked Olliphant, starting his cross-examination.

'He'd have had a better chance still,' said the witness, 'if he'd stayed at home that day.'

'But when he came round the bend he could have seen the car, couldn't he?'

'He was entitled to assume that it would stop.'

'Never mind what you consider he was entitled to assume,' replied Olliphant. 'He could have seen it, couldn't he?'

'Yes, if he'd looked.'

'You say it was coming fast, don't you?'

'Certainly.'

'And the motor-cyclist – how fast was *he* going?'

'At a very moderate speed.'

'So that if the motor-cyclist doing this very moderate speed had looked he would have seen a fast car about to come across his path?'

'Yes.'

'Well, then, the motor-cyclist, going at this only moderate speed, could simply have avoided the accident by stopping and letting the car go in front of him?'

'He didn't have to expect there was a maniac on the road.'

'But, if you do see a maniac on the road, you don't deliberately have a clash with him, do you?'

'I've never met a maniac, and I've never had an accident.'

'I'm glad to hear it, but, if you saw a maniac charging in front of you, you'd very quickly have an accident if you didn't stop, wouldn't you?'

'I don't see what that's got to do with the case.'

'That will be for the Bench to judge. Now, if this motor-cyclist was going at a *very* moderate speed – and those are your words, Mr Salter – can you think of any reason why he shouldn't have stopped and saved himself from the consequences of the dangerous driving of the accused? I should make it plain that I'm not accepting for a moment that my client was driving dangerously, or that he didn't stop at the "halt" line, but – assuming that he did all these things – why on earth d'you think the motor-cyclist did not stop, if he was going at a very moderate speed?'

'I suppose he didn't see the car in time.'

'But once he was round the bend it was in full view.'

'It was to his side.'

'But in full view and approaching fast in front of him.'

'Yes.'

'It sounds a bit odd, doesn't it? The motor-cyclist didn't want an accident, did he?'

'Of course not.'

'Well, if what you've said is right, he appears to have had one quite unnecessarily.'

'He hadn't much time.'

'He had ample time if he was going at a *very moderate* speed. Of course, if he was going fast, and my client wasn't, that might have accounted for it, mightn't it?'

'He was *not* going fast, and the accused *was*,' persisted the witness.

'I gather you drive?' asked Olliphant.

'Yes.'

'Ever ridden a motor-cycle?'

'Yes.'

'If you'd been on the motor-cycle what would you have done?'

'How can I say?'

'Can't you? You'd have braked, wouldn't you?'

'Possibly.'

'Certainly, surely, if you'd seen the car?'

'I suppose so.'

'And if you were only going at a *very moderate speed* you'd have had time to stop, wouldn't you?'

'Possibly.'

'So that *you* wouldn't have had the accident.'

'If I hadn't seen the car, I would have.'

'But not if you had seen it?'

'Probably not. It depends when I saw it.'

'It's the duty of all motorists to keep their eyes open, isn't it?'

'Of course. But they can't look everywhere at the same time.'

Andover got up.

'I haven't objected to this line of cross-examination so far, but I submit it is quite irrelevant. My learned friend knows perfectly well that, even if the motor-cyclist was guilty of negligence – by not looking or by not braking in time or even – though that isn't the evidence – or even by going too fast, that is no answer to a charge of dangerous driving by the accused. If it is true that the accused came across the "halt" line without stopping and drove straight on to these dangerous cross-roads, the negligence of the other driver, if any, has nothing to do with this charge. It would only be material in a civil case – and this is very far from being a civil case.'

'I'm obliged to my friend,' said Olliphant, 'but my case is going to be that the accident was entirely caused by the negligence of the motor-cyclist in coming round the corner too fast. My client had stopped at the cross-roads. He then perfectly properly advanced on to the cross-roads and . . .'

'Is my learned friend making a speech or cross-examining?' asked Andover.

'I'm making a speech – I hope a short one – in reply to your own,' said Olliphant. 'As I was saying when I touched some sensitive part of my friend's intellectual physiognomy, as I was saying, my case is that my client, having stopped at the "halt" line, came perfectly properly on to the cross-roads – he couldn't go fast as he was only just starting – when the motor-cyclist came round the corner too fast to be able to stop. At the moment I am cross-examining the witness to try to establish that is what happened. I can't ask more than one question at a time, and what I've been doing, which apparently upsets my learned friend, is to deal first with the motor-cyclist's behaviour.'

'His behaviour doesn't matter if your client didn't stop at the "halt" line,' said Andover.

'But it does if my client *did* stop. I really don't know why my learned friend is so sensitive about my questions. Possibly he's just trying to show that he's awake.'

'That's highly offensive,' said Andover.

'I apologize,' said Olliphant.

'Very well,' said Andover.

'Mr Olliphant and Mr Andover,' said the chairman. 'These interchanges between you are not uninteresting, but could you both please remember that we are laymen, and, though we have the advantage of being advised by a most learned clerk, he cannot continuously interpret to us what you are saying to each other. You have now been bickering for about two minutes and none of us on the Bench has the faintest idea what it's all about. We should, therefore, be obliged if, when either of you gets up to make some kind of statement in the middle of the examination or cross-examination of a witness, you would explain to us – I repeat, to us – what exactly is going on. After all, we're dealing with the case and, unless we know what you mean, you might as well save your eloquence until you have a jury to try to influence. Even as a layman I can understand that, when a case is being tried before a jury, counsel may sometimes think it is to his advantage to interrupt his opponent when questioning a witness – either to score a point or to blunt a point made by his opponent. But we are not trying the case, gentlemen. All we shall be concerned to say at the end of all the evidence is whether or not there is a case to be tried. There are, I gather, a good number of witnesses to be called. This will inevitably take some time, but it will take very much longer if you gentlemen are going to indulge in what, from our point of view, are unintelligible verbal polemics. I would not for a moment suggest, as some people might, that you are endeavouring to prolong the hearing for as many days as possible for your own pecuniary advantage, as I am sure that that is very rarely done by advocates in this country and certainly not by counsel of your standing. But, realizing that that cannot be the case and not being able to understand what the reason for your behaviour is, I find myself compelled – both on my own behalf and on behalf of the other members of the Bench, to ask you both either to explain in simple intelligible language what is going on between you or . . .' and here the chairman paused for a moment and then very clearly and precisely added: 'or stop it.'

Olliphant and Andover looked at each other, at first like schoolboys caught out of bounds and then perhaps more like elderly uncles caught by young nephews eating jam out of a jar in the larder. The chairman had touched them both on tender spots. Both of them were barristers of complete integrity and considerable experience, but neither could resist a verbal tussle if the occasion offered. There are members of the Bar who can keep absolutely quiet during a case, except when it is necessary for them to speak in the interests of their clients. But they are few. This is not because, as the chairman pointed out, speech is more golden than silence in the Courts – only a minute percentage of advocates would even think of this – but because they cannot resist the opportunity of talking. This is not solely a characteristic of lawyers but, by reason of the fact that much of their livelihood depends upon speech, they get more opportunity of indulging in it.

It would indeed be possible for counsel on one side to make bets with his solicitor or his junior upon how many times he could make his opponent get up and say something. If this game is to be played it is suggested that there should be no score if the interruption is legitimate. And, to give the game more interest, it might be possible to put barristers into classes. Thus, if you can get Mr Binks to interrupt without sufficient cause three points should be scored, whereas, in the case of Spinks, one point might be too much. There would have to be other rules too. For example, no point would be scored if you actually invited your opponent to speak. For instance, if you say 'Would my learned friend be good enough to tell me whether he objects to such-and-such,' even the most silent of counsel must reply. No points for that. It would be interesting to observe how far counsel would go in playing such a game. For instance, in the case of a silent, affable and calm opponent, who is sitting looking blandly in front of him during your address, without a hint on his face of what is going on in his mind, could 'My learned friend may scowl as much as he likes,' be used legitimately to try to bring him to his feet? And if he denied the accusation should a point be scored? Certainly, if unexpectedly he jumped angrily to his feet and said that hitherto he had only with difficulty restrained himself from interrupting such a gross travesty of the facts, two points would be scored. And, of course, once you had jerked him into verbal activity, a further point would be scored each time you prodded him with effect. A variant of the game would be played between opposing counsel to see who could make a silent judge talk. But impertinence would be a disqualification. Nor would a point be scored by a direct question to the judge which required an answer. Conversely a game might be played to keep too-talkative judges quiet. This would either have to be scored by the minute – or in extreme cases by the half- or quarter-minute – or it could be scored by the question or sentence. How many questions can you ask the witness without the judge intervening? Or how many sentences can you speak without an interruption? Again there would have to be rules. For instance, if a judge interrupted, that would score a point. But if at the end he said:

'Mr Brown, I'm afraid I interrupted you,' it would lose a point to say:

'Oh, my Lord, it is so helpful of your Lordship. It is so much easier for counsel if he knows what is going on in your mind.'

The chairman who presided over the Needham Bench was a dentist. One of his colleagues, a woman, kept an antique shop, and the other was a works manager. They formed a very efficient Bench, doing their work conscientiously and with good humour. The chairman seldom spoke or interrupted and his long speech to counsel was quite a surprise to his colleagues. He had thought on the lines on which he had spoken for some years, and at last he felt he must let himself go.

'I feel better now,' he whispered to Mrs Fernhead, the antique dealer.

'Well done,' whispered the works manager.

The clerk rather wished he had said it all, but on consideration he felt that he could not very well have delivered a homily of that kind. Moreover, being a lawyer, he may have instinctively felt that if he attacked counsel, they might both turn on him and rend him apart. No, it was the chairman's job and beautifully he had done it. But there was one thing *he* could do. There had been complete silence for a second or two after the chairman's speech, though it seemed much longer. The clerk beamed at both counsel and, in his most affable voice, said to Olliphant:

'Have you finished your cross-examination, Mr Olliphant? No? I'm sorry,' and, smiling pleasantly, he looked down at the paper on which he was writing the depositions.

'Your next question then, Mr Olliphant, please,' said the chairman, equally pleasantly.

'Mr Salter,' said Olliphant, 'in your opinion could the motor-cyclist have avoided the accident by stopping if he'd seen the car as soon as he came round the bend?'

'Possibly.'

'Why not certainly?'

'How can I be certain? The whole thing was over in a second or two.'

'So you're not certain?'

'No.'

'Because it was all over so quickly?'

'Yes.'

'Of what are you certain beyond the fact that there was an accident?'

'I'm certain it was the car's fault.'

'That you have made fairly obvious, but, without intending to be offensive, your opinion is not what is wanted. It is your evidence of what you actually saw that I am asking you about. What *did* you actually see apart from the collision?'

'I saw the motor-cyclist come round the bend.'

'But not sufficiently to judge whether he could have stopped? Did you see the car before the collision?'

'Of course I did. I saw it cross the "halt" line.'

'You must have been looking at it then?'

'I was.'

'Are you saying that it crossed the "halt" line at the same time as the motor-cyclist came round the corner?'

'About the same time.'

'Then, if you were looking at the car, how could you have seen the motor-cyclist?'

'I looked from one to the other.'

'Why?'

'I can't tell you. Why does one do anything?'

'Perhaps you expected an accident?'

'I can't say. It's possible.'

'You are certain of the movements of the car, but not of the motor-cycle?'

'Why d'you say that?'

'Because you say you watched the car cross the "halt" line, but you didn't see the motor-cyclist long enough to judge his speed.'

'He was going at a moderate speed.'

'Now we're back where we were a few minutes ago. If that is correct he could have stopped in time, but you're not certain whether he could have stopped in time or not. Therefore, you cannot be certain of his speed.'

'He did all he could.'

'Are you certain of that?'

'Of course I am.'

'Then why did you say to me a few moments ago that you weren't certain whether he could have stopped or not?'

'Because I wasn't.'

'Then you can't be certain that he did everything he could.'

'Well, I am.'

'Thank you, Mr Salter. That's all I wish to ask,' said Olliphant.

'No re-examination,' said Andover, and the second witness's evidence was concluded.

Chapter Seven

At the Bar of the Blue Goose

As Michael and Andrew walked away from the Court, Andrew was very pleased with the result of the first day's proceedings.

'If those are their two best witnesses I don't think you've much to fear.'

'What was all the talk between counsel about this not being a civil matter, and the motor-cyclist's negligence being irrelevant? I should have thought it was most relevant.'

'Well, in a way no,' said Andrew. 'You see, if you crossed the "halt" line without stopping that was obviously a dangerous thing to do and, even if the motor-cyclist came too fast without looking, your dangerous driving would have been *a* cause of the accident. And that would be enough to do you down.'

'Then why are you so cheerful?'

'Because this last chap's obviously unreliable. He's tied himself in knots. No one's going to convict you on that evidence.'

'But there are all the others.'

'Oh – I know. I'm only saying the first two aren't up to much. And you must bear in mind that Olliphant hasn't opened up yet. Without bringing his big guns into play he's shown they're poor witnesses.'

'But what else will he do at the trial?'

'My dear fellow, what else? Don't you realize that he hasn't at the moment directly attacked their statements that they saw you cross the "halt" line? That's the vital part of the case, and that's he's leaving till the jury can hear the cross-examination. The chances are that the chap will go into the box ready to deal with the questions he's been asked today and will find he's got to meet quite a different line of questioning.'

'Well, let's hope the others are all the same. It's quite vital I should get off. Apart from any consequences to myself, if I were sent to prison it would kill Sheila. I know it.'

'How is she, and how are they managing about the newspapers?'

'She's as well as we can expect, I suppose. But there's no question of newspapers at the moment. I wish there were. But I have arranged that they'll be terribly careful about that if – when she asks to see a paper. If only I weren't an M.P. it wouldn't be so bad. Probably wouldn't be reported except locally or at the end perhaps. But, as it is, every day at the Magistrates' Court and every day at the trial will be reported. I can't blame the Press. It's reasonable enough. But it's very worrying. How long d'you think it'll be before I go for trial?'

'That depends. If they keep on adjourning for a week at a time, as they have today, it'll be some weeks, but I expect they'll give you a couple of days together so as to avoid these adjournments. They need more Courts and more magistrates and, until they have them, there'll always be delay in these Courts. Anyway, try and forget it for the moment. Come to my flat and have a drink.'

While they were having a drink in Andrew's flat Colonel Brain was having one in the Blue Goose.

'Nasty case that you're in, colonel,' said the landlord. 'Seeing he's an M.P. and all that.'

'Being an M.P.,' said the colonel, 'does not give you a right to run over people, whatever else it does.'

'I agree with you there, colonel, but I always think it's a pity when a prominent man gets charged with something like this. It's bad for him and it's bad for us. Now, if it had happened to someone like you and me, no one would worry about it.'

'It's expected of us, you might say,' said the colonel. 'Otherwise the death and injury rate might go down. 'Pon my word, you know, I think I've said something there. We're all accepting this business of death on the road as a normal incident of daily life. Inevitable, like lightning, we think. Look at the paper. "Three killed in crash." What d'you do? Say – "Oh, what a disaster?" Go to church and pray? Send a subscription to something or other? Determine to drive more carefully yourself? Not a bit of it. You hardly notice the paragraph and call for another pint. Which reminds me. Same again, please.'

'A pint it is,' said the landlord, and drew one and handed it to the colonel. Colonel Brain took a long draught, put the mug down, wiped his lips.

'It's good, your bitter, landlord,' he said. 'The best I've known. But not like it was in my father's day. That's one of my regrets. That I've never drunk pre-1914 beer. A very different part of speech. That was beer. This is hardly more than water. Coloured water. Can't think why we drink it.' He finished the mug and handed it back to the landlord. 'You were saying something, landlord,' he said.

'Oh – just about the accident. I shan't do much trade on the day of the trial. Most of my customers are giving evidence, I believe.'

'Well, I am for one,' said the colonel. 'And pleased to do so. A disgraceful case, if ever there was one. I'd disqualify him for life and send him to prison for a year. That'd teach him to drive across cross-roads, M.P. or no M.P.'

'Prison's a bit hard for a man like that.'

'A coffin's a bit harder, landlord. And that's where the other fellow might have been. No fault of the M.P. that he wasn't. There's plenty of scope in prison. Libraries and entertainments, and I don't know what. Some people think they do too much for the people inside prison and too little for those outside. But there's one thing you can't argue about. There's no scope in a coffin. That's final. All the same, when I go I shall take a book with me. Just in case.'

'A bit dark?' queried the landlord.

'You're right,' replied the colonel. 'And a pocket torch.'

'What about the life of the battery?'

'That's a point,' said the colonel. 'I suppose they wouldn't allow you to have it wired up. No, that's troublesome. It hadn't occurred to me.'

'Why not read the book now?' said the landlord, 'and then you won't have to take it with you.'

'What book?'

'The book you want to take.'

'But I don't know what it is.'

'Can't you find out, colonel?'

'I could, I suppose,' said the colonel. 'Who d'you think I should ask?'

Other customers of the Blue Goose that morning were also witnesses who were to be called.

Mr Salter was there, a Mr Berryman, a Mr Stuart, who had been driving behind the motor-cyclist, and a middle-aged man called Samuel Piper who said he'd been standing outside the Blue Goose at the time of the accident. They soon began to discuss it and Mr Salter told the others what had happened during his cross-examination, as the evening papers only reported a small portion of his evidence. He also warned them that Olliphant was a dangerous cross-examiner.

'He'll try to make you say the motor-cyclist was going too fast,' he said. 'I nearly got had by that, but not quite.'

'But I'm not a-following how he can make you say something you do not a-want to say.'

Mr Piper spoke in a curious manner. His voice was neither cockney nor bucolic, but he had a curious unidentifiable accent and a habit of putting an 'a' before some words and an unnecessary 'of' at the end of a sentence.

'You'll soon find out if you take that attitude,' said Mr Salter.

'I am not a-taking any attitude,' said Mr Piper. 'I am simply not a-following.'

'These lawyers can make some people say anything.'

'But how?' persisted Mr Piper. 'If I say a car was black, how can they a-make me say it was a-white?'

'You think it was black, do you?' said Mr Salter, putting his thumbs in the top of his waistcoat and striking the attitude of a lawyer cross-examining.

'I a-do,' said Mr Piper.

'I put it to you it was white.'

'Well, it was a-black.'

'White.'

'A-black.'

'White.'

'A-black.'

Mr Salter took his thumbs out of his waistcoat and had a drink. His first attempt at cross-examination was not so far very successful. But he was not to be defeated so easily. He replaced his thumbs and went on:

'Let me ask you something else. How could you tell what colour it was?'

'By a-looking at it.'

'Could you see the colour quite plainly?'

'Quite.'

'And you think it was black?'

'No.'

'Oh,' said Mr Salter, 'you don't think it was black?'

'No.'

'Then it was white?'

'No.'

'But either it was black or white. You're not suggesting it was grey?'

'No.'

'Well, if it wasn't black, it was white?'

'Yes.'

'Well, if you don't think it was black, it was white.'

'No.'

'I put it to you, sir,' said Mr Salter, taking one hand out of his waistcoat and pointing his index finger at Mr Piper, 'I put it to you that you are trifling with the Court. You admit it was either black or white and that you don't think it was black. Then it must have been white.'

'No.'

'Explain yourself, sir.'

'You asked me if I a-thought it was black and I said "No, I didn't think it was black."'

'That's right. You did.'

'Well, it's true I didn't a-*think* it was black. I *knew* it was.'

'Oh,' said Mr Salter, 'I don't think you'd be allowed to do that in a real Court.'

'But it's still a-black,' said Mr Piper. 'I want to know how they can a-make you say it's a-white.'

Mr Salter tried again.

'Could you have made a mistake, sir?' he asked.

'Yes,' said Mr Piper.

'You admit that?'

'Yes, I could have made a mistake. But I didn't. It was a-black. Perhaps,' he added, 'you'd like to ask me if black doesn't sometimes look the same as white?'

'That's a silly question.'

'But I'd answer "yes" to it,' said Mr Piper.

'That black sometimes looks the same as white?'

'Often,' said Mr Piper. 'In the dark, you know.'

'Ah!' said Mr Salter, 'was it not dark on this occasion?'

'Yes,' said Mr Piper.

'Then how could you tell whether it was black or white?'

'Because the a-street lights were on,' said Mr Piper.

'I give in,' said Mr Salter. 'But I'm not a trained lawyer. You wait till you're facing this chap Olliphant. I reckon I gave a pretty good account of myself, but I admit I had some nasty moments. He nearly made me say that, if I'd been the motor-cyclist, there wouldn't have been an accident.'

'If I'd a-been the car driver there certainly wouldn't have a-been one,' said Mr Piper.

Chapter Eight

A Drive in the Country

The prosecution called in all a further seven witnesses, Mrs Benson, Mr Piper, Patricia Gaye, Joan Anderson, Mr Berryman, Mr Stuart and a retired naval officer, Commander Parkhurst. The driver of the motor-cycle was still too ill to give evidence, but Andover stated that, as far as they could tell, he would be called at the Central Criminal Court if he were well enough and notice would be given to the defence of the effect of his evidence. Michael was duly committed for trial. He had to wait for four weeks before the case was due to be heard.

It was on a Saturday that he learned that Mr Justice Grampion was to be the judge at the Old Bailey. He at once told Andrew, who consoled him as best he could. On the Sunday he suggested that, after Michael had seen his wife at the hospital, they should drive out into the country for a change and have lunch.

'Help to take your mind off the case,' he said. 'But, of course, it won't. Still, it can't do any harm.'

Michael agreed and on the Sunday Andrew picked him up at the hospital in his car. To begin with they talked about the trial, then about Sheila, and then about the trial again.

'Where are we going?' asked Michael.

'There's quite a good little pub at Grantley. D'you know it?'

'No. Where is it?'

'It's not far. Get you back to the hospital by four.'

'O.K. That'll be fine.'

They drove on for a few miles and then the car started to slow down as the engine cut out.

'Damn,' said Andrew.

'What's happened?'

'It's the carburettor. I'll be able to fix it.'

He got out, lifted up the bonnet and had a look round.

'Give me the screwdriver out of the cubby-hole, old boy, would you?' he said after a few moments.

'There isn't one,' said Michael after looking.

'Oh – it'll be in the boot.'

Andrew went back to the boot and opened it, but there was no screwdriver.

'Damn!' he said again. 'What the devil's happened to it?'

'P'raps it's in the side pocket,' said Michael.

But it was not.

'Never mind,' said Andrew. 'There's a house over there. I expect they'll lend us one. Come along.'

Michael got out and they went towards the house.

'Nice little place,' said Michael. 'Wonder who lives here?'

'A stockbroker I should imagine,' said Andrew. 'But we'll soon know. Or shall we? We can't very well ask.'

Andrew knocked and a moment or two later the door was opened by a middle-aged man.

'I'm so sorry to trouble you, sir,' said Andrew, 'but have you by any chance a screwdriver you could lend us? We've had a breakdown.'

'Certainly, if I can find one. Come in.'

'It's very good of you, sir,' said Andrew.

'We're most grateful,' added Michael.

'Not at all. Wait a moment.' The man went away and left them standing in the hall.

'Seems a nice chap,' said Andrew.

'I've a feeling I know his face,' said Michael.

'Have you? Means nothing to me.'

A moment later the man returned with a screwdriver, which he handed to Andrew.

'Here you are.'

'Thank you very much, sir. Could you tell me if we're far from the William Arms?'

'About five miles,' replied the man. 'Second turning on the right after the church.'

'It's a pretty good pub, isn't it?' asked Andrew.

'The food's quite good,' replied the man.

'We're having a last fling,' said Andrew. 'My friend here's going to lose his licence on Monday.'

'Indeed?' said the man coldly.

'Yes, he's being tried before old Grampion at the Old Bailey. Hasn't a hope in front of *him*. No motorist has.'

'Indeed? I *am* old Grampion. Kindly return the screwdriver when you've finished with it.'

'I'm terribly sorry, sir,' said Andrew. 'I'd no idea.'

'Good morning to you,' said Grampion.

They walked back to the car.

'Gosh, now we've done it,' said Michael. 'What a chance! I could see him add on six months for your crack.'

'If he tries the case,' said Andrew.

'What d'you mean *if*? He's going to.'

'Is he? Mightn't our little – purely fortuitous – interview make him ask whether you've any objection to being tried before him? Judges are very careful about such things, I fancy. They'll never preside at a trial if somebody might think there was prejudice of some kind.'

'Gosh,' said Michael. 'Now I know why you suggested Grantley.'

'I've always heard the beer's good at the William Arms,' said Andrew. 'Let's have a smoke and then you take this back to him. He'll remember your face better.'

'Didn't you want to use it?' asked Michael.

'I'll just try the starter once more.'

The car started immediately.

'But what'll happen now?' asked Michael.

'If I'm not very much mistaken,' said Andrew, 'Mr Justice Grampion will ask if you have any objection to his presiding at your trial; your learned counsel will ask you; you will say you have and Olliphant, whilst assuring his lordship that he personally would be only too delighted for his lordship to try the case – the liar – will say that, in the circumstances, you would prefer to be tried by another judge. Grampion will agree and they'll give him a case from another judge's list and send yours to the other judge.'

'But can't we get into trouble?'

'How? Nobody except us knows that I did it on purpose. I suppose it might be contempt of Court deliberately to talk to a judge as I did, but I wouldn't know about that. But no one in the world can prove I knew he was a judge. Even you only felt you'd seen him somewhere before. It is a coincidence, it's true. But that's all they've got against me. There's nothing against you, because you didn't know till afterwards. Oh no, you're safe enough. And so am I. And it was easy, wasn't it?'

'Suppose he doesn't say anything and just goes on with the case?'

'Then one of us will ask Olliphant to object because of what's happened today. And, after all, it's not unreasonable not to want to be tried before a judge whom you've recently insulted. Justice must manifestly be seen to be done. How can it be if you've just given the judge a metaphorical black eye? I can't see a judge sticking to his guns if you persist. But you must do that, if necessary. And, by Jove, it'll be worth it. He's the only judge I'm frightened of. Even Olliphant mightn't be able to get between him and the jury. And if they did find you guilty before him, you'd be for it all right. It's horrible to think of. No, my little plan had to be put into action. And I'm sure it'll work.'

'If I say "thank you", will that be compounding a felony?'

'I wouldn't know that, either, because I don't know what a felony is. But I rather doubt it. Anyway, I won't tell.'

They had lunch in a much happier frame of mind. Mr Justice Grampion's description of the food at the William Arms was as fair as his judgments, and certainly more satisfactory in the circumstances to Michael and Andrew.

Chapter Nine

Mrs Benson Makes Two Calls

In spite of the fact that Mr Justice Grampion concentrated on motoring cases, it was quite a good day for the public at the Old Bailey and it had no reason to grouse at the fare provided. Trials of Members of Parliament are rare. Even if all they've done is to charge down a motor-cyclist and injure him seriously, the fact that the result of the case could mean ruin to the man in the dock, or an end to his political career, would do a good deal to make up for the banality of the crime. After all, real tragedy is a very agreeable spectacle for some people, and, if you don't have the luck to see a man who has the possibility of being hanged, you can make do quite well with the spectacle of a public man, up till recently well known for his speeches in the House of Commons, about to be placed in a prison cell and to consort with cut-throats, pickpockets and fraudulent tricksters. Prisons are not such cruel places as they were in the days of Oscar Wilde. But those with imagination can still get some considerable interest by visualizing the possibility of a man – normally seen exchanging friendly greetings with his friends in the Palace of Westminster – walking round a prison exercise yard instead. And the great thing about it was that it was only a possibility. The suspense was there all the time. Not guilty and he goes back to Westminster. Guilty and it's Wormwood Scrubs. Not with every judge, perhaps, but with Mr Justice Grampion it was a certainty. It was not surprising that Michael went white when he was first told who his judge was to be.

But there was going to be a nasty shock for the public. After Michael had surrendered to his bail and the clerk was about to swear in the jury to try him, Mr Justice Grampion intervened.

'Just one moment, please,' he said. 'Mr Olliphant, before your client pleads to the charge, I should like to know whether he has any objection to the trial taking place before me. By a pure accident I met the defendant and a friend a day or two ago, and something was said which makes it desirable that I should ask the question.'

'Thank you, my Lord,' said Olliphant. 'I had no idea of this. I'll take instructions.' He went to Michael and whispered: 'What's all this about?'

'Tell him I do object,' said Michael.

'Yes, but what happened?' asked Olliphant.

'Does that matter? We called him names, and I *do* object.'

Olliphant went back to his place.

'My Lord,' he said, 'I am most grateful to your Lordship for giving me that opportunity. If I may say so with the greatest respect, those of us who know your Lordship know quite well that nothing that may have taken place a few days ago would make the slightest difference to the way in which your Lordship would preside at this trial . . .'

'Then your client has no objection?' interrupted the judge.

'I was saying, my Lord,' replied Olliphant, 'that I would certainly advise him not to object, my Lord . . . we at the Bar all know . . .'

'Yes – yes, thank you, Mr Olliphant,' said the judge, 'but the defendant is not at the Bar. Do I gather that he would feel more comfortable if some other judge presided?'

Andrew said to himself: 'Much. Much more comfortable.'

'My Lord,' said Olliphant, 'so far as I personally am concerned, I'm sure your Lordship will understand . . .'

'Mr Olliphant,' interrupted the judge again, 'there's no need to be embarrassed about it. If the defendant would prefer another judge he shall have one.'

'Will your Lordship allow me to take further instructions?'

'No, Mr Olliphant. If your original instructions were to object, I should be very sorry to try any case where the accused himself felt that he was starting off on the wrong foot.'

'It's very good of your Lordship.'

'It is neither good nor bad, Mr Olliphant,' said the judge. 'It is the way justice is administered in this country. And let me say at once that it is no fault whatever of the defendant that this has happened. It was a pure accident. Perhaps Judge Benbow will be able to take the case. I hear that his list is finished. At least – I suppose your client's car hasn't broken down near his house too?'

The case was accordingly transferred to Judge Benbow, one of the additional judges, and shortly afterwards Michael pleaded 'Not Guilty' to the charge, and Andover opened the case. He opened it in much the same way as he had opened it at the Magistrates' Court. He stated the short facts, announced who his witnesses were going to be, explained that the motor-cyclist, although happily almost fully recovered, remembered nothing of the occurrence, and then he called his evidence.

It had been agreed that, in view of her age, he should call Mrs Benson first, and that she should then be allowed to go to a friend's flat from where she could be summoned at short notice if she were needed again. The day of the accident had certainly been a rather important one for Mrs Benson. There was more than one reason. On that day she had kept an appointment with her solicitor, Mr Callander. He had almost retired from practice, and his means were ample to provide him with a comfortable retirement. But he missed the office and in consequence used to come up every now and then and choose a client to while away the time. There was a marked difference in the way in which he treated such clients from the way in which he used to treat his clients when he was in full practice. In those days he was very busy, got to the point immediately and refused to gossip. People came to him because he was efficient, not because he had a good bedside manner. He won their cases but not their hearts, and, after all, that was what they wanted. But, until his reputation was fully known, many of his clients were a little disappointed at their first interview.

'Cruel, was he? Where did he hit you and who saw the bruises?'

'He was that mean.'

'So am I, madam, but I don't hit my wife. In this Court it's no bruises, no case. Well, where were they?'

Mr Callander of course realized that it was not essential in law for a husband to hit his wife in order to be guilty of cruelty. But he also knew that anything short of physical violence usually meant simply that the parties did not get on well together. He further knew that such was the view of his Bench. A couple of black eyes, a bruised arm, and an independent witness to at least one of them – not just 'my mum' who had always hated the man anyway – and Mr Callander could almost guarantee success. But meanness, or too much or too little affection, he turned away regularly. Sometimes clients took his advice and made the best of things. Sometimes they went to other solicitors and in due course lost their cases.

By his efficiency and hard work, Mr Callander built up a large local practice. His brusqueness was not due either to pose or natural surliness. He simply wanted to save time. He made sure that he got down to the essentials, but he developed a natural talent for eliminating at a very early stage anything that was irrelevant, however important it seemed to the client. Later on it became a habit, and all his regular clients knew that, if he said he would see them for ten minutes, they would normally be out of his office within that time. At the zenith of his career he could see six clients in an hour when another solicitor would see only one or two.

But, as soon as he had all day to spend on his task, he liked to spend it, and those of his old clients, who did not realize the reason for his curtness before he retired, soon learned it after his retirement. They discovered that it was useless calling on him unless they were prepared to spend the whole of the morning or afternoon in his office. The result in the end was exactly the same, except that they had to spend two or three hours with him instead of ten minutes. He charged no more and his advice was just as good, but he was then in practice as a form of enjoyment and he made certain that he had it. Those of his clients who were in too much of a hurry to humour him could go to his younger partner, or take their business elsewhere.

At the time Mrs Benson went to see him he was well over eighty, but his memory for law was good and, though he sometimes confused one client with another for a short time, the mistake was always put right before the end of the interview.

'Ah, Mrs Benson,' he said. 'How nice. How very nice. We don't see enough of each other. I remember saying that to one client once. She wasn't at all pleased. She only came when her husband had been knocking her about. I used to get her a separation order on an average about once every two years. She used to go back to him, you see. Obviously she liked being knocked about up to a point. But, when that point was reached, she came to me. And she was a picture. She knew what I wanted. And she came with them on her. When the photographer opposite saw her come into my office he was over himself in two shakes. Wonderful pictures he used to take. From every angle. I've never known a man who could make so much of a black eye. In black and white, I mean. But when he started to use colour, it was a treat, Mrs Benson, I assure you. You should have seen the Bench passing along the photographs to each other. The husband had no chance with those photographs. Never had to call *her* mother. Shouldn't have liked to. I strongly suspected that her husband could have got a separation on the ground of assault too. But never got the chance of photographing him. Well, this is very nice, Mrs Benson, and how are your bruises?'

'Mine?' said Mrs Benson, quite shocked. 'How on earth did you know about them?'

'My little joke, I'm afraid. That's all. But I'm sorry to hear that you have bruised yourself. I do it myself. It's falling down, isn't it? D'you know, each morning I get up I say to myself: "Now, I'm not going to fall down today – I'm not, I'm not, I'm not." And then, as long as I remember,

I'm all right. But then, of course, one has other things to think about. And down I go. And it's so painful, Mrs Benson, so very painful. It's the only time I wish I were a woman. They say you don't feel pain as much as we do. But perhaps it's simply that you don't make so much fuss. I make an awful fuss, I can tell you. If there's someone about, that is. No use if one's by oneself. I hope your fall wasn't serious?'

'Oh, nothing really. I just fell up the stairs and bruised my knee.'

'Fell *up* the stairs, did you. Well, that's better than falling down them. If you've come to make another will, better make it quick before you do fall down them. Now, that's a thing I'm always careful about. You can't forget you're walking downstairs. And I hold on tight. More than one client I've had who ceased to be one by falling downstairs. So glad you fell up them, Mrs Benson. Is that why you're here by any chance? Want to sue someone about it? Not a very good bet up the stairs, Mrs Benson. Now down – with a stair-rod out or the stair carpet rucked up, and your eyes being none too good – down would be a different proposition, but then it might be your executors suing and that wouldn't help you much, would it, Mrs Benson? No, I believe in sticking to life while we can still get around and we haven't gone potty. Mind you, if I thought I was going potty, I *would* fall down the stairs or something like that. That's no life at all. But I'm glad to say I've nothing to complain about in that respect. And I'm enjoying life, Mrs Benson. I hope you do too. I'm sure you do.'

'As a matter of fact, that's why I've come to you, Mr Callander. Can you get me my licence back?'

'Licence? Licence? Oh – of course. Oh dear. You want to drive again. D'you think it wise? I've given it up, you know. Seen too many mishaps. As a matter of fact it was after your little affair that I gave it up.'

'But, Mr Callander, I love it so. It means so much to me. It makes me feel so independent. I didn't go fast at all. Just jogged along. I couldn't do any harm. Please, please, couldn't you get it back? I'm sure if you asked the magistrates for me, they'd give it me.'

'They'd make you take a test, you know.'

'But I could get through that all right, I'm sure.'

'After all this time, d'you think? It must be quite six months since it happened, isn't it?'

'Well, yes it is. But I've sort of . . . sort of kept my hand in – only in an imaginary sort of way, I mean. If I'm being driven I imagine that it's me driving – unless it's in that horrid little fast thing of my grandson's. Then I close my eyes and hope. But when Fred or Robin (my sons, you know) are taking me out I pretend to myself that it's me. And I swerve and put on the brake and slow down and stop and put my hand out and everything. In my mind, I mean. And then, when I look out of the drawing-room window and see cars going by, I do the same. Though *I* wouldn't drive like some of them. They're not safe on the road, not half of them. So you see, Mr Callander, I have kept my hand in. I'm sure I'd pass the test all right.'

'Exactly how old are you, Mrs Benson?'

'Well . . . I've gone eighty.'

'Yes, I know, Mrs Benson, but how far gone?'

'Only two years.'

'Eighty-two. Well, I'm a year older.'

'Even you drove after my age, Mr Callander – for a whole six months. You must have. Look, if you'll get me my licence back, I'll promise to give it up when I reach your age. Promise faithfully. Just give me six months more. You don't know what it would mean to me.'

'Well, I can't hold out much hope, Mrs Benson. The Bench intended it to be for life. They told you so. But we can apply.'

'And perhaps you and I could just go out for a short ride in your car. And you could let me sit in the driving seat and hold the wheel and things . . . not while it was going, of course . . . unless – unless . . .'

'Now, Mrs Benson,' said Mr Callander, 'if I didn't know you so well, I'd have thought you were inciting me to commit a criminal offence – me, a solicitor. Do you realize what would happen if I let you drive my car and we were caught?'

'Suppose we weren't!'

'Mrs Benson, we *should* be caught. I should insist on your driving to the police station and giving ourselves up. And then d'you know what would happen? We would both go to prison and I should be struck off the Roll.'

'I was only joking, of course, Mr Callander.'

'I hope so, Mrs Benson, indeed I do. But such a joke makes me wonder whether I should be justified in applying to the Bench for you.'

'Oh, but, Mr Callander, a joke amongst friends. I may call you a friend, mayn't I?'

'Even if I don't make the application, Mrs Benson?'

'Oh, but you will – you will. Even if it should fail, you will try. Promise?'

'Have you seen your doctor recently, Mrs Benson?'

'Well, he saw my knee.'

'It was as bad as that, was it. I'm sorry. Is it quite better?'

'Are you thinking of your photographer, Mr Callander? Did he really photograph such things?'

'You'd be surprised, Mrs Benson. But you must go to your doctor and see if he'll say that in his opinion you are physically and mentally fit to drive a car.'

'Oh, how wonderful it sounds. Fit to drive a car!'

'But he may not say it, Mrs Benson. Doctors are far more prone to say that people are unfit for something than that they're fit. It's so much easier.'

'But you're going to try, Mr Callander, you're going to try?'

'If you'll get me a certificate from your doctor first, and if he'll be prepared to go into the witness-box to support it, I'll put in an application.'

'Oh, I could kiss you, Mr Callander.'

'Not while you're driving, Mrs Benson.'

On the way home from Mr Callander, Mrs Benson suddenly had a bright idea. First she called on her bank manager to see how much she had in her current account and then went into Mrs Fernhead's antique shop.

'Ah, good morning, Mrs Fernhead, I didn't expect to find you here this morning. I thought you'd be administering justice.'

'Oh, we do have our days off, you know. I only sit on Mondays, Wednesdays and Fridays, unless anyone's ill or on holiday or there's some emergency.'

'Of course, how silly of me,' said Mrs Benson. 'Otherwise it'd be a full-time job. But I think it's wonderful of you anyway to give up so much time. And it's all for nothing.'

'Well, someone's got to. But I like it anyway.'

'Our neighbour Mr Chase says that, if it weren't for people like you, it would cost the country hundreds of thousands, I'm not sure that he didn't say millions of pounds a year more to run the Courts.'

'Well, it's nice to feel of use.'

'Mr Chase says that most of the criminal work in the country is done by you.'

'You'll make me feel quite conceited.'

'You've something to be conceited about, Mrs Fernhead. Running a family and a shop and sitting in Court at least three times a week – I think it's quite wonderful of you. I suppose,' she added, 'you could sit any day if you wanted to?'

'How d'you mean?'

'Well, if there were a particular case you were interested in which was on a Thursday, for instance, you could arrange to sit, if you wanted to? I mean if I were on the Bench, and I knew there was a particularly interesting case coming on, I'd like to be there.'

'Oh – I expect it could be arranged. You're not thinking of any particular case?'

'Oh, good gracious, no,' said Mrs Benson hurriedly. 'Now, I mustn't take up your time gossiping. And I didn't come here for that. I've got a lot of presents to buy and I want your help, Mrs Fernhead.'

'Oh, how nice. We've had a slack week. I hope you're going to be extravagant.'

'Now it's funny you should say that,' said Mrs Benson. 'That's exactly what I am going to be.'

'Golden wedding, perhaps, or shouldn't I ask?'

'No, it's just old age. I was walking along the street, thinking of nothing in particular – I'd just been to see Mr Callander – to pass the time of day and he kept me talking – and I suddenly saw an old man crossing a pedestrian crossing. And all the traffic waited for him. And I said to myself – I suppose they don't think he's worth killing off. It's too bad the way motorists keep people waiting at those crossings. When I drove, I always stopped for them, unless I was in a hurry, of course. But most drivers take not the slightest notice unless they're made to. I make them all right. I hold up my umbrella and off I go. But I always say thank you, mind you. I give them a sweet smile both sides. But I was telling you. I saw this old man walking across and I wondered how much longer he'd got to live. And then I did the same for myself.'

'You've years to go yet, Mrs Benson.'

'Perhaps I have. Perhaps I haven't. But the point is, what am I going to do with them? What's the good of having a little money in the bank? I can't go and look at it. And, anyway, I'm not a miser and running gold sovereigns through my hands wouldn't give me any pleasure, let alone dirty pound notes. Or clean ones, for that matter. So I said to myself – Mrs Benson, why don't you go and spend some? Why not? I said. So here I am.'

'Well, Mrs Benson, I think it's a wonderful idea. And I'm glad you've chosen me to begin with.'

'To begin with? Forgive me, d'you mind if I sit down? I find walking very tiring. Very tiring. To begin with, you say? Oh, no – I shall begin and end here. After all, there's nothing nicer than giving away things, and you've got something for everyone. So I'm going to give them all a nice surprise. And you're going to help me, if you will.'

'With the greatest of pleasure, Mrs Benson. Have you made up your mind how many things you want and how much you want to spend altogether? If you can tell me that, I'll be able to make suggestions that will fit in with your ideas.'

'How kind you are.'

Mrs Benson thought for a moment or two. The most she had ever spent at Mrs Fernhead's shop was about five pounds.

'A hundred and fifty pounds,' she said, and noted with pleasure that Mrs Fernhead had to stifle a gasp of astonishment.

'Well, that does give us a little scope,' she said after she had got over the shock. 'I think we should be able to give some nice surprises with that. Who shall we start with?'

'My eldest son, of course. First things first. What a charming man Mr Callander is. Does he appear much in front of you these days?'

'Not very often. But we do see him occasionally.'

'Is he as good as ever?'

'I think he's a very wise man. Of course I've only been on the Bench five years. So I didn't know him before he retired. But he always has something sensible to say, even if we disagree with it.'

'D'you often disagree with him?'

'Oh, naturally. It depends on what his case is. But, however bad it may be, he always seems to find a point worth listening to. If there's anything at all to be said for his client, he finds it.'

'Then he doesn't win all his cases?'

'Good gracious no. No lawyer does that. For one thing it wouldn't look well if he did. People would say he had the Bench in his pocket. But we don't decide against him merely to show that we're independent. It's bound to happen that way with a reasonably good Bench. And, leaving myself out of this, I think I can fairly say that our people are pretty good.'

'I'm sure they are, Mrs Fernhead, and you too.'

'How nice of you. Now, what about your son's tastes? He doesn't collect snuff-boxes by any chance?'

'No, but he might like to start. D'you think that would be a good idea?'

'Well, you could always try and I'd be pleased to exchange it for something else if he didn't like it.'

'What a good idea, and how kind of you. D'you think

Mr Callander wins more of his cases than any of the other lawyers?'

'Well, you see, he only appears occasionally now, as I've said. So it's difficult to say.'

'Who would you say was the best of your regular lawyers?'

'Oh, that's easy – young Mr Fenton. We call him young, but he's nearly sixty. His father used to be Clerk of the Court, and so his son has always been young Mr Fenton. Oh, yes, he's very good. A very smart man. I remember once in a shoplifting case he borrowed a pen or pencil from the prosecuting solicitor and slipped it into his pocket. Then in his final speech to us he pretended that he thought he heard his opponent say something. "No," said his opponent, "I didn't say anything." "Oh!" said young Mr Fenton, "I thought you might have been asking for your pencil back," and out he brought it. "You see how easy it is, your Worships, and I hope no one in this Court thought I was trying to steal it."'

'And did the man get off?'

'Well, it was a woman. No. We fined her forty shillings.'

'Well,' said Mrs Benson, 'what was the point of having young Mr Fenton with all his tricks and sleight of hand, if he didn't get her off?'

'Well, to tell you the truth, he very nearly did. But I stuck out for a conviction and eventually I brought them round. Now, what d'you think of this? It's rather expensive, I'm afraid, but it's a genuine Louis Quinze.'

Mrs Benson looked at it without the interest which she affected to assume.

'It's charming,' she said. 'Did it really belong to the Emperor? How can they prove it?'

'Oh, it's just the century. It didn't belong to – to the Emperor, so far as I know. Of course it might have. It might have belonged to anyone.'

'Yes, of course, how stupid of me. What are you like with driving cases, Mrs Fernhead – I mean you, yourself?'

'Well, I'm afraid I'm rather bad. It's one of my faults.'

'I see,' said Mrs Benson, in a rather dejected tone. 'No,

I don't think I like that very much. And, as you say, it's probably too expensive. When I said a hundred and fifty I was probably making it too much. More like a hundred. Or perhaps fifty would be more sensible. You mean you convict them all?'

'Oh, no,' said Mrs Fernhead. 'My fault – and I admit it is one – my fault is that I'm always saying: "It might have been you. That's just the sort of thing you'd do." So I'm afraid I'm inclined to let them off. I don't mean in very serious cases. But in minor ones. You know the sort of thing – not looking quite enough, not stopping quite soon enough, not giving a signal. All those little mistakes we all make.'

'I see,' said Mrs Benson. 'Let me see that snuff-box again. You mean that, on the whole, you let them off if you can.'

'Well, I oughtn't to say this perhaps,' said Mrs Fernhead, 'but I'm very like a juryman with motorists. You know the way the lawyers complain that juries always let off motorists. Well, I'm afraid I'm much the same as the juries. I've seen the superintendent look at me sometimes, after we've let someone off in a driving case. Or not disqualified them when he thought we ought to have done.'

'You mean you're against disqualifying drivers?'

'Oh, certainly, unless one has to. It's far worse than a fine or even imprisonment for a lot of people. It stops some people from earning a decent living. And it stops others from so much enjoyment. You can hardly do anything without a car these days. I'm sure I don't know where I should be without one.'

'You know,' said Mrs Benson, 'I think I'm going to have this snuff-box after all.'

'I'm afraid that, if your limit is fifty pounds, you won't be able to. It's marked seventy pounds. I could put it in at sixty guineas, but I'm afraid that's the very least I could do it for. So we'd better have a look for something less extravagant. You've all the other things to get, too.'

'No, Mrs Fernhead,' said Mrs Benson resolutely. 'It's our privilege to change our minds and I'm going to exercise it, and hang the bank balance. I can't think what made me become so mean all of a sudden. I said a hundred and fifty pounds and I'm going to stick to it. I must say I do admire the way you try your cases. How human. How very human. I wish people could know how you considered every point of view so carefully. I'm sure that most of the public think that you take a joy in convicting people and taking away their licences. Now *I* at any rate know different.'

'Of course,' said Mrs Fernhead, 'I don't want you to get the wrong impression. Some people *have* to be kept off the road. People who aren't safe.'

'I see,' said Mrs Benson, fingering the snuff-box. 'What sort of people d'you mean?'

'Oh – wild young men who obviously are going to drive dangerously if they drive at all.'

'I couldn't agree with you more,' said Mrs Benson, putting down the snuff-box. 'Now, what next, something for my daughter-in-law, d'you think?'

'What about those two dogs? They're real Staffordshire. I could let you have them for – let me see – as you're having the snuff-box – just a moment – yes, I could put them in at forty pounds for the two. And, of course, people who are too old or infirm to drive.'

'What did you say?' said Mrs Benson.

'Forty pounds for the two,' said Mrs Fernhead.

'Too much,' said Mrs Benson. 'But what did you say about old people?'

'Some of them can hardly walk, let alone drive.'

Mrs Benson picked up the snuff-box again and was wondering how to say it when Mrs Fernhead went on:

'People much older than you, I mean,' she said. 'You've no idea of the age some people think they can still drive safely at.'

'No, indeed,' said Mrs Benson. 'How old?'

'We had an old man of ninety the other day.'

'Ridiculous,' said Mrs Benson. 'He might have died as he drove along.'

'Just as the chairman said. "His engine would have been more likely to give out than the car's," he said. Not in public, of course. Wouldn't want to hurt the old man's feelings.'

'How did the case come before you?'

'Fortunately the old boy had had a slight accident. Nothing serious. But enough to give us jurisdiction to take away his licence.'

'And quite right, too,' said Mrs Benson. 'At ninety I shouldn't expect to have a licence. Personally, I would say that anyone over eight-five was suspect.'

'I quite agree,' said Mrs Fernhead.

'But up to that age it depends on the driver. If her health – if his health,' she corrected herself, 'is all right and he's driven for – well, shall we say . . .' she paused for a moment while she calculated how long she'd been driving – 'for thirty years or more, then I don't see why she – he shouldn't go on driving for several years more. Do you, Mrs Fernhead?'

'Of course, every case depends on its own facts, but, speaking generally, I entirely agree with you, Mrs Benson.'

'Forty pounds, I think you said,' said Mrs Benson. 'I think that's very reasonable. Let me see, that leaves us a hundred pounds about, doesn't it?'

'Only fifty, Mrs Benson. The snuff-box is sixty-three and the two dogs forty. That's a hundred and three. Call it a hundred and that leaves fifty?'

'Call it a hundred,' said Mrs Benson, 'and we'll have another hundred. I'm enjoying myself.'

'So am I,' said Mrs Fernhead. 'Something for the grand-children, did you say? They'll be more difficult. What are their tastes?'

'Some old people get a lot of pleasure from driving, Mrs Fernhead,' said Mrs Benson, 'and, as you said before, to take away their licences unnecessarily may be worse than a prison sentence.'

'So long as they're safe to themselves and to other people, I don't see why they shouldn't go on till eighty-five or so,' said Mrs Fernhead. 'Now, what about a small jewel case? I've an enchanting little thing here.'

'How d'you decide whether a person's safe or not?' asked Mrs Benson.

'Here it is, charming don't you think? They're semi-precious stones. Fifteen guineas. How do we decide whether they are safe? Well, if they don't have any accidents, they're safe on the face of it.'

'But suppose they have a small accident, just a small one?'

'Sometimes it's a matter of luck whether an accident's small or not. Another half inch and there might have been a death.'

'But you can have an accident without anyone being at fault.'

'You can, but not very often. On an icy surface, perhaps. But usually someone's to blame.'

'Then d'you mean that if an old person – under eighty-five, I mean – had had one accident you'd take away his licence?'

'Oh, not necessarily. As I said, it depends on the circumstances. If he wasn't too old, and it was an accident any of us might have had, we'd probably give him the benefit of the doubt.'

'I think the case is charming. And so cheap. I'll have it, but I'd like to give her something else as well.'

'Well, now, Mrs Benson, I don't want to be naughty or to tempt you too much – but I suppose you're very fond of the girl?'

'She's a darling. I looked a bit like her when I was a girl.'

'Well, I know I shouldn't,' said Mrs Fernhead, 'but this necklace – isn't it sweet?'

She held it up. Mrs Benson took it from her.

'I can see her in it. I must have it.'

'But I haven't told you the price. And I can't even reduce it. It's on sale or return.'

'Never mind, she's a dear girl. How much?'

'It's eighty-five pounds, I'm afraid. Actually,' she added, 'that would just make up two hundred.'

'So it would,' said Mrs Benson. 'Well, that's done then. But I've forgotten the boy.'

'But we've reached the limit, Mrs Benson. I mustn't let you overspend. I should feel guilty.'

'Mrs Fernhead, it's very good of you,' said Mrs Benson, 'but after the way you behave in Court, I'm not surprised you're just as considerate in your own shop. But it's my money and I'm going to spend it. How much is that paper-knife?'

'Well, that isn't terribly expensive. Just five pounds.'

'Right,' said Mrs Benson. 'I'll give you a cheque.'

'I hope I'll be seeing you again soon,' said Mrs Fernhead.

'May be sooner than you think,' said Mrs Benson. 'As a matter of fact, I'm applying for my driving licence back again.'

'Are you really then?' said Mrs Fernhead. 'I do hope you get it.'

'How kind you are,' said Mrs Benson, as she handed over the cheque.

'I don't know whether it'll be on one of your days,' she added.

'I'll make a point of coming down,' said Mrs Fernhead, 'if you'll let me know.'

'Oh, Mrs Fernhead, I wouldn't have suggested such a thing.'

'Not at all, I'll be only too pleased. And I do hope you succeed. Of course you'll understand, I shall only be there to listen. Knowing you as I do I couldn't possibly take part in the case or talk to any of the others about it. But . . . Well, good-bye – Oh!'

For Mrs Benson had left, slamming the door.

But nevertheless in due course she obtained a certificate from her doctor and Mr Callander issued an application for the return of her licence. It was to be heard shortly after Michael's trial began.

Chapter Ten

Mrs Benson in the Box

It will be understood that, in the circumstances, as Mrs Benson walked into the witness-box she felt vaguely apprehensive – as though it were a dress rehearsal for the application for the return of her licence. Indeed, from time to time she had difficulty in concentrating on the accident about which she was being asked and almost believed she was being examined or cross-examined about her application.

From the moment she had taken the plunge and induced Mr Callander to make the application, she had thought of little else. She had taken a little time to get over her first disappointment at having spent £200 with Mrs Fernhead, only to find that she had wasted her money, but even that set-back was only temporary. After all, while it would have been nice to have squared one member of the Court – no, 'squared' didn't sound very nice – to have worked on – no, that wasn't too good either – to have softened up – certainly not – to have conditioned – no – influenced – no – bribed – no, how horrible – no, perhaps it was just as well that her little idea had not borne fruit. She would sleep happier as it was. She was very wrong to have thought of the idea even, let alone to have put it into effect. But it was on the spur of the moment. And such sins are more easily forgiven. And, after all, she only thought of the idea as she walked away from Mr Callander, and she had carried it out before she had really considered the implications. Tampering with justice! Dreadful thought. After eighty blameless – well comparatively blameless years – to bribe or try to bribe a judge, that was pretty bad. No, she was glad the attempt had failed. Now, if she got her licence back her conscience need not trouble her. It would have been done fairly and properly.

So Mrs Benson consoled herself for her little lapse, as she would have described it. It also gave her some slight consolation to think that it was still just *possible* that Mrs Fernhead *might* put in a word for her with one of the justices who *would* be hearing the application.

But now she must try to concentrate on the accident. She walked into the witness-box and took the oath. She then accepted the judge's invitation to sit down. Andover, counsel for the Crown, examined her and she found it easy to answer his questions. Had she seen the accident? Yes, clearly. Had the defendant's car stopped at the 'halt' line? No, definitely. Could the motor-cyclist have avoided the accident? Certainly not. If only my own application goes as easily, she thought.

When Andover sat down after his short examination of her, Mrs Benson, after the manner of many witnesses, got up and started to leave the witness-box.

'Just a moment, please, Mrs Benson,' said the judge. 'Mr Olliphant will want to ask you some questions.'

'Oh, of course. I'm sorry, my Lord,' she said, and walked back and sat down again. Why had she forgotten cross-examination? she asked herself. She had read about cross-examination many times. She had even wondered whether it would be the police superintendent who would cross-examine her or some lawyer when she made her application, and here she was forgetting all about it and starting to go away. How lucky to have a dress rehearsal. It would have been awful if she'd walked away at her own case. They might have thought she was frightened of being asked questions. That wouldn't do at all.

'No, I'm not frightened at all,' she said out loud in answer to Olliphant's first question, which had been:

'I apologize for asking, but how old are you, Mrs Benson?'

As she said the words Mrs Benson heard the actual question and quickly added:

'I'm not frightened to give my age, I mean. When I

remember it, that is. I get confused sometimes with the dates.'

'Of course,' said Olliphant soothingly, 'one's memory does play one tricks, doesn't it, sometimes?'

'My memory's all right,' said Mrs Benson. 'It's just dates.' And then she found herself adding: 'And I can read a number plate at twenty-five yards without glasses.'

'Wonderful,' said Olliphant. 'I congratulate you, Mrs Benson.'

'Thank you,' said Mrs Benson.

'Now perhaps you wouldn't mind telling me the question I just asked you?'

'One's memory does play one tricks sometimes, doesn't it?' said Mrs Benson. She was starting to enjoy herself. But her enjoyment was short-lived. The judge did not like witnesses to enjoy themselves. That is not to say that he did not want to put them at ease. That was quite a different matter. But he knew that, once a witness was allowed to be smart or to play for laughter, the answers might be dominated by the desire to obtain such laughs rather than to forward the inquiry into the truth.

'Mrs Benson,' he said sternly, 'please don't be flippant. This is a Court of Law and this is a very serious case.'

'I'm sorry, my Lord,' said Mrs Benson fearfully. She could almost see her application for the return of her licence being dismissed there and then. Well, this was another lesson she had learned. No flippancy.

'What *was* the first question Mr Olliphant asked you?' went on the judge.

Everything went out of Mrs Benson's head. She only knew that she was frightened. Eventually she found her voice.

'I've – I've forgotten, my Lord,' she murmured.

'That's quite all right,' said Olliphant, smiling, 'I'm often just as bad. I'm afraid I asked you a very rude question about your age.'

'Oh, of course.' Mrs Benson was finding Olliphant a very pleasant cross-examiner, as indeed he intended that she should. How nice it would be, she thought, if he appeared on my application. Perhaps he will.

'I'm eighty-three next birthday. Or is it eighty-two?' she added.

'I'll settle for eighty-two,' said Olliphant, 'and that's five years more than I thought.'

I wonder if there's some way of getting him into my case, thought Mrs Benson. The same little imp which had induced her to walk into Mrs Fernhead's was at it again. Before long she would be treating Olliphant as though he were acting for the police in her own case. Well, there was no harm in being pleasant in her answers.

'Eighty-two,' repeated Olliphant, 'and with eyesight as good as ever. I do congratulate you.'

'Thank you,' said Mrs Benson.

'And your hearing excellent too?' asked Olliphant.

'Perfect.'

I wonder if he knows about my application, she wondered. Is he asking these questions in this case to put me off my guard? After all, good hearing and good sight were vital to her if she was to succeed in her own application. The ways of the law were unknown to anyone except lawyers. Perhaps this really was how it was done. Well, she was quite all right so far.

'Just dates not too good?' went on Olliphant.

'No,' admitted Mrs Benson. They couldn't possibly refuse you a licence because you were bad at dates.

'So you mightn't remember the date of the accident, for instance?' asked Olliphant.

'It was the ... no the ... no, I forget.'

'It was the 12th December as a matter of fact,' said Olliphant.

'Of course,' said Mrs Benson.

'You really remember it?' asked Olliphant.

'Now you mention it, I do,' said Mrs Benson.

'But I'm not good at dates either,' said Olliphant. 'Suppose I've made a mistake? I don't say I have – but suppose I have, would you be able to tell me?'

'I don't quite follow,' said Mrs Benson.

'Are you quite sure the accident was on the 12th?'

'If you say so, yes,' said Mrs Benson.

'But if I said it was the 13th you'd be equally sure?'

'Well, I suppose so.'

'That means, doesn't it,' said Olliphant, 'that you're not really sure when it was?'

'I'm sure that what you'd say would be right,' said Mrs Benson. She was determined to be nice. Even if he weren't in her case, there'd be no harm in being nice. And there always was the chance that he *would* be in it.

'You're very trusting,' said Olliphant. 'I hope you'll accept a few things from me before we've finished. Let's start with your hearing.'

Mrs Benson prepared herself. It *was* her case he was after.

'Your hearing is excellent. So I expect you heard the sound of the collision?'

'Certainly I did.'

'Was it a loud bang?'

'Yes, it was.'

'Didn't it frighten you?'

'Well, it was startling.'

'Naturally enough,' said Olliphant. 'You heard a bang, you were startled, you looked up, and saw the accident?'

'That's right,' said Mrs Benson.

'That was at least three, and possibly four questions rolled into one,' said the judge. 'It won't do, Mr Olliphant. Mrs Benson, did you see the car moving before the collision?'

'Oh, yes, my Lord.'

'Did you see the motor-cyclist hit the car?'

'Oh, yes, my Lord.'

'Yes, Mr Olliphant,' said the judge.

'Why were you startled?' asked Olliphant.

'Anyone would have been,' said Mrs Benson.

'Quite so – but was it the bang which startled you?'

'I suppose so.'

'But you knew there was going to be a bang.'

'Certainly not,' said Mrs Benson firmly.

'But if you saw the motor-cyclist and the car approaching

each other, you must have seen there'd be a collision and that would mean a bang?'

'It all happened so quickly,' said Mrs Benson.

'Of course it did. And I suggest that from your point of view it started with a bang.'

'Well, there *was* a bang.'

'And it was the bang which made you look?'

'Well, I was looking.'

'At what?'

'I was just looking.'

'At anything in particular? Before the accident, I mean.'

'I wouldn't say anything in particular.'

'What were you thinking about at the time, Mrs Benson?'

'Thinking about? Oh – I couldn't say now.'

'Try to think, Mrs Benson. What had you done that day?'

Oh, good gracious, thought Mrs Benson, he's going to ask me about Mr Callander – and – and Mrs Fernhead. What shall I say? Oh dear, this *is* difficult. I must be very careful. This *must* be about the case. Why should he ask me what I was doing, if it isn't?

'Well, Mrs Benson?'

'I must think.'

'Take your time, Mrs Benson. It was the day of the accident. Never mind the date. Just think what had happened that morning.'

Mrs Benson still hesitated. Well, she thought, there can't be any harm in saying I went to see my solicitor. So she said it.

'I don't want to pry into your private affairs,' said Olliphant, 'but was it about something important?'

Something important! Something important! Almost the most important thing in the world. After health *the* most important.

'Well, it *was* important,' she conceded.

'Then you must remember what it was about?'

'Yes,' said Mrs Benson, 'I do.'

'Now, I don't want to know what you told your solicitor, or what he said to you, but can you give me an idea of the subject matter?'

This is it, thought Mrs Benson. What shall I say? He knows, anyway. And that old judge too. They all know. It's a shame questioning an old woman like this. Making a fool of her. Playing with her. Suddenly Mrs Benson became angry.

'You know very well,' she said.

'Indeed I do not, madam,' said Olliphant.

'Liar,' said Mrs Benson.

'Mrs Benson,' said the judge, 'you will at once apologize to learned counsel. I won't have this behaviour in my Court – even if you are eighty-two.'

'I'm sorry, my Lord,' said Mrs Benson, her anger turning almost to tears. 'But you all know what it's about and it's a shame to tease an old woman.'

'What on earth are you talking about, madam?' asked the judge. 'What is it you think we all know?'

'About my licence,' sniffed Mrs Benson.

'What about your licence, and what sort of licence?' asked the judge.

This really is too bad, thought Mrs Benson. What sort of licence indeed! As though there were any other kind of licence she could want. She said nothing.

'What kind of licence?' persisted the judge.

'Driving licence of course,' said Mrs Benson sulkily.

'There's no "of course" about it,' said the judge. 'But you'd gone to see your solicitor about your driving licence, had you?'

'Yes,' said Mrs Benson still sulkily.

'It's no good getting cross,' said the judge. 'It's my duty and counsel's duty to inquire into these matters. If he asks anything he shouldn't, I shall stop him.'

'I wouldn't have come here if I'd known,' said Mrs Benson.

'You have to come here,' said the judge. 'You're under subpoena.'

'Well, it isn't fair,' said Mrs Benson.

'What isn't fair?' asked the judge. 'Any citizen who sees an accident must give evidence about it, if necessary. You gave your name to the police.'

'I wouldn't have.'

'I dare say not, but you did. And that's all there is to it,' said the judge. He was a little tired of Mrs Benson. 'Yes, Mr Olliphant?'

'I'm sorry my questions trouble you, Mrs Benson,' said Olliphant, 'but just tell me this, if you will? You were consulting your solicitor about your driving licence, were you?'

'Well, yes.'

'Had it lapsed or something?'

'Well, in a way – yes.'

'I see. And you wanted to know if you could get it renewed?'

'Yes.'

'And that was important to you?'

'Yes.'

'Why?'

'I like driving.'

'I see. And what did you do after you'd seen your solicitor? What did you do?'

'I bought some presents.'

'That took your mind off your driving licence, did it?'

'Not exactly,' said Mrs Benson, trying to be as truthful as she could.

'How much did you spend?'

'Quite a lot.'

'About how much?'

'About £200.'

'Are you a rich woman, Mrs Benson?'

'Not rich, no.'

'Was £200 a lot for you to spend on presents?'

'Yes, it was.'

'Wedding or something?'

'No.'

'Then what was the occasion for your spending so much?'

'I wanted to.'

'Of course, but why?'

'I just wanted to.'

'But had you ever spent anything like that sum on presents before?'

'I don't think so.'

'Then there must have been some reason for your doing it all of a sudden?'

'I just felt like doing it. When you're my age things happen like that. You suddenly think – I may not be here tomorrow, so I'll have some fun today.'

Mrs Benson was quite pleased with that explanation.

'And did you find it fun?'

'I enjoyed buying the presents.'

'And did you think how pleased your family would be with them?'

'Yes.'

'Particularly as they were unexpected?'

'Quite.'

'And you were on your way back from seeing your solicitor about your driving licence and buying these expensive presents when the accident happened?'

'Yes.'

'What were you thinking about immediately before the collision – the licence, or the presents?'

'The licence.'

'Are you sure? The licence only costs 15s. The presents cost £200.'

'Well, it might have been the presents.'

As a matter of fact it had been the presents. At the moment of the accident Mrs Benson was seething with indignation at Mrs Fernhead for taking £200 and calmly telling her, in effect, that it wouldn't help her to get her licence back.

'Weren't you imagining the pleased faces of those of your family for whom you'd bought the presents? That was half the fun, wasn't it, Mrs Benson? Half the fun imagining how pleased they'd be and the other half seeing how pleased they actually were? No, I'm sorry. A third of the fun actually buying the presents and a third each the other two things I've mentioned.'

Mrs Benson said nothing.

'That's it, isn't it?' asked Olliphant.

'You go too fast for me,' said Mrs Benson. 'I don't quite follow.'

'It's my fault,' said Olliphant. 'I'm sorry. I'll take it more slowly. Mrs Benson, when one is walking along the road one usually thinks of something. Often it's something quite unimportant, such as what you are going to have for dinner or whether to write to a friend or something of that kind. D'you understand so far?'

'Yes,' said Mrs Benson doubtfully.

'Just like today, Mrs Benson,' said Olliphant. 'If you came to Court alone you were probably wondering what it would be like in Court – or what questions you'd be asked.'

'Yes,' said Mrs Benson, still doubtfully. She was wondering where the catch was. She felt sure that she was being coaxed into laying her head upon the block and that suddenly the knife would come down and cut it off.

'Well, now,' said Olliphant, 'if one has just done something interesting, such as – such as seen a good film or play, or called on a great friend, or bought some expensive presents for someone, the natural thing for most people would be to think about it immediately afterwards.'

'I think I see what you mean,' said Mrs Benson.

'Good,' said Olliphant. 'You'd be thinking – will my grandson like the . . . tool-set I've bought him, will my niece like the necklace, and so on?'

'Well, I might have been.'

'You weren't thinking of traffic accidents?'

'Oh dear no.'

'Exactly. You weren't thinking of driving?'

'Well, I was, as a matter of fact.'

'Why?'

'Because I like it.'

'But you can drive any day. Why bother to think about it?'

Mrs Benson was silent.

'Oh – I see,' said Olliphant, 'you couldn't drive any day, because you hadn't a licence. Is that it?'

'Yes, in a way,' said Mrs Benson.

'So you were thinking about driving again?'

'Yes.'

'Not about other people driving, but about you yourself driving?'

'Yes.'

'And then there was a bang, and that interrupted your thoughts?'

'Yes.'

'It still won't do, Mr Olliphant,' said the judge, 'though you have improved. That was only two questions rolled into one. Mrs Benson,' he went on, 'before the bang, did you see the motor car?'

'Yes, my Lord.'

'Did you see it cross the "halt" line?'

'Yes, my Lord.'

'Did it stop at the "halt" line?'

'No, my Lord.'

'Yes, Mr Olliphant,' said the judge.

Olliphant sighed.

'Mrs Benson,' he asked, 'seeing the car coming along – if you saw it – didn't interrupt your thoughts, did it? You were thinking about driving – you were imagining yourself at the wheel of your own car?'

'Yes.'

'And then there was a bang?'

'Yes.'

'And that interrupted your thoughts?'

'Yes.'

'So that, right up to the moment of the bang, you were imagining yourself in the driving seat of your own car?'

'Yes.'

'Then the bang came?'

'Yes.'

'And then you thought only of the poor motor-cyclist who was injured?'

'I suppose so.'

'Where was he?'

'Lying on the road.'

'You just saw him lying there?'

'I can't be sure. I think so.'

'And after the accident you talked to other people who'd seen it, I suppose?'

'Yes.'

'And they told you what they'd seen, and you told them what you'd seen?'

'Yes.'

'And you were all sorry for the poor motor-cyclist?'

'Yes, of course.'

'And the car drove off?'

'Yes.'

'So I suppose you were all angry with the driver of the car?'

'Wouldn't you be?'

'Yes, indeed,' said Olliphant. 'I should, particularly if I couldn't get his number. Thank you, Mrs Benson. That is all I wish to ask.'

'Mrs Benson,' asked the judge, 'are you quite sure you saw anything before the bang?'

'How d'you mean, my Lord?'

'You've told me you saw the car come across the "halt" line.'

'Yes, my Lord.'

'Are you sure you really did see it then, or was the first thing you knew when the accident had actually happened?'

'I think I saw it, my Lord.'

'But it was all over very quickly?'

'Oh, yes. In a flash.'

'Exactly. Just one other thing, Mrs Benson. You say you want to drive again. D'you think it wise at your age to start again?'

'Oh, yes, my Lord,' said Mrs Benson anxiously.

'This accident case we're trying might have ended in a death. As we get older our reactions get slower. You'd be very upset, wouldn't you, if you were responsible for someone else's death?'

'But I wouldn't be, my Lord. I'd never drive like he did, my Lord. I'm very, very careful. If you'd come with me, my Lord, I'd show you. I really am terribly careful, my Lord. I promise I'll never have an accident.'

'That will do, Mrs Benson. Thank you.'

'But please, my Lord,' went on Mrs Benson feverishly, now convinced that the whole case was a put-up job to keep her out of her licence. 'Please give me back my licence. I never drive more than thirty miles an hour. And I'll be extra careful all the time. But it does mean so much to me, my Lord.'

'Thank you, Mrs Benson. That will be all.'

'But will you give it me back, my Lord?' said Mrs Benson. 'It's all I've got in the world. It's my one great pleasure. I haven't got so long to live, my Lord, and you wouldn't want to deprive me of my pleasure. Everybody has a car today, my Lord, and ...'

The judge held up his hand.

'Please,' he said, 'that will do.'

'Then I may have it back, my Lord?' Hope suddenly came to Mrs Benson. 'Oh, thank you, my Lord.'

The judge was tempted to let someone else point out the misunderstanding, so that he could persuade her to leave the witness-box, but better instincts prevailed.

'I'm afraid your licence has nothing to do with me, Mrs Benson.'

'Nothing to do with you, my Lord?' said Mrs Benson incredulously. 'But what about all these questions you've been asking me?'

'I'm afraid,' said the judge, 'I only asked them in the hope of persuading you not to drive any more. We see so much of accidents and of the terrible consequences that it's natural that we shouldn't want anyone whose driving might be ... might be – entirely due to age, of course – might be not too – let me put it another way. We don't want anyone driving whose reactions might not be quite fast enough.'

'But come with me, my Lord, and you'll see. I'll prove it to you,' said Mrs Benson.

'It's nothing to do with me,' said the judge. 'If you can persuade the authorities to let you drive, it's their responsibility – not mine.'

'Then you're not refusing me?'

'I've no power to refuse or to permit,' said the judge. 'I was just expressing a personal view.'

'And all this has nothing to do with it?'

'Nothing at all,' said the judge.

'And I can still make my application?'

'You can make any application that the law allows, madam,' said the judge.

'Oh, thank you,' said Mrs Benson. 'Thank you.'

'There's nothing to thank me for, madam,' said the judge. 'I am only telling you what the position is.'

'I'm so grateful, my Lord,' said Mrs Benson. 'And may I tell them that you said I could apply?'

'You may tell them nothing of the kind,' said the judge. 'You go to your solicitor, and he'll tell you what you can say and what you cannot say. But you *mustn't* say I'm supporting your application.'

'But I don't have to say that you're against it?'

'No, Mrs Benson, you don't. Now please leave the witness-box.'

'Thank you, my Lord,' said Mrs Benson, and did as she was told.

Later that day she went back to Mr Callander and told him as well as she could what had taken place in Court.

'Have I spoilt my chances, d'you think?' she asked anxiously.

'I don't think so,' said Mr Callander. 'The Bench will decide on what happens in *their* Court, not in someone else's. But they'll certainly want you to take a test. That's the best you can expect. And that'll mean one thing.'

'What?'

'That at least you'll get one more drive.'

Chapter Eleven

Colonel Brain Again

The next witness was Colonel Brain. As he entered the witness-box he looked at the clock. When the clerk was about
to administer the oath to him he said:

'Excuse me a moment, sir.'

Then he took out a notebook and made an entry in it.

'What are you doing?' asked the judge.

'Making a note of the time, my Lord.'

'Why?'

'I once heard the Lord Chief Justice tell a witness to look
at the clock, and later on he asked him a question about the
time. So I thought I wouldn't take any chances, my Lord,
and wrote it down. My memory's not so good as it was.'

'Kindly take the oath,' said the judge.

The colonel did as he was told, and then looked expec-
tantly at prosecuting counsel. Having regard to what had
happened at the Magistrates' Court, Andover tried to frame
his questions in such a way as to give Colonel Brain as little
opportunity as possible for straying from the issue. Having
successfully asked him the necessary formal matters he came
straight to the point.

'On the 12th December last there was an accident between a car and a motor-cycle, near the Blue Goose public
house. Did you see anything of it, Colonel Brain?'

'Yes, sir, I did.'

'Address your remarks to my Lord, please.'

The colonel frowned.

'I will try, sir – my Lord I mean. But it's very difficult to
look at one person and talk to another.'

'I agree,' said the judge. 'As far as I am concerned, so
long as you speak up, you may look at whom you please.'

'Thank you, my Lord,' said the colonel.

'And continue to say "My Lord" and not "sir",' said counsel.

'I don't mind what you say,' said the judge, 'so long as you speak clearly and intelligibly and truthfully. Personally – and I speak with deference to other learned judges – I think this business of "turn to my Lord when you answer my questions" is ridiculous. It must be difficult enough to give evidence at all. First of all the witnesses – in many cases – are frightened by the length of the oath and its exact wording, and just as they're trying to remember what they're going to be asked about they are reprimanded by counsel for looking at *him* when they answer *his* questions. Colonel Brain is perfectly right. It *is* very difficult to look at one person and speak to another, and I don't expect it in this Court.'

The colonel bowed to the judge.

'Thank you, my Lord,' he said. 'This is a better start than the one I had when I came here last time.'

'But,' said the judge, 'I don't approve of witnesses being garrulous or frivolous.'

The colonel slipped his hand into his waistcoat pocket and brought out his little book. He took a quick look down.

'Gabbling, gassy, windy,' he said.

'What on earth are you doing?' asked the judge.

'Just seeing all the things I mustn't be,' said the colonel, 'non-stop, voluble, running on – it's quite right, my Lord, I am inclined that way.'

'Well, you will kindly confine yourself to answering the questions shortly while you're in this Court,' said the judge.

'Shortly,' mused the colonel. 'You mean that I should leave something out in order not to say too much?'

'You know perfectly well I don't mean that,' said the judge. 'I mean that you shouldn't indulge in the verbal antics which you appear to enjoy.'

'Verbal antics,' said the colonel. 'I've never been told that before, my Lord. Verbal antics. But it's rather a nice expression.'

The colonel got out a pencil and was about to write in his notebook when the judge interrupted.

'Stop,' he said. 'If you go on playing the fool, colonel,' he went on, 'it will be my painful duty to send you to prison.'

The colonel looked sadly at the clock, and then down at his notebook. Although he actually said nothing out loud, it was plain that he was indicating that within ten minutes of his going into the witness-box he had been threatened with prison.

'My Lord,' he said, 'I mean no disrespect. If you will consult with the Lord Chief Justice – not the present one, but the last one to retire – oh, no, my Lord, I'm terribly sorry – the one I mean has retired too far – he said the same to me but he never sent me to prison in the end. I think he understood. If your Lordship will just indicate to me when I go too far, I'll stop at once. I assure your Lordship I'd do a great deal to avoid going to prison. It's this box, I think. It does things to a man.'

'Go on, please, Mr Andover,' said the judge.

'What did you actually see, colonel?'

'I saw the collision, sir – my Lord. I forget which it is.'

'His Lordship says either will do,' said Andover.

'Tell me frankly,' said the colonel, 'which would you personally prefer?'

'Colonel Brain,' said the judge, 'I fine you £10 for contempt of Court. The price will go up next time.'

'How far?' asked the colonel.

'£50,' said the judge. 'That will be £60 in all. The next time it will be prison.'

The colonel looked sadly at the clock. Then he started to feel for his wallet.

'I doubt if I've got that much on me, my Lord,' he said.

'You can pay later,' said the judge.

'Thank you, my Lord,' said the colonel. 'All the same,' he added, 'this is going to be a pretty expensive visit. It's the season, I suppose,' he added sadly.

The judge tapped his pencil and the clerk got up and held a whispered conversation with him.

'Can't he help it?' asked the judge. 'I don't want to send him to prison if I can avoid it.'

'Nobody does,' said the clerk, 'but I was warned about this by the Magistrates' clerk. They actually considered whether to have a motion in the High Court to commit him.'

'I see,' said the judge. 'I suppose he *can't* help it. If necessary we'll have him examined by a doctor. If I have to commit him, that is.'

Then he said aloud:

'Go on, Mr Andover, please.'

'Did you see anything before the actual collision, Colonel Brain?' asked Andover.

'Yes, sir,' said the colonel.

'What did you see?'

'A number of things, sir.'

'What were they?'

'In what order would you like them, my Lord?'

The colonel had hit on the bright idea of saying 'sir' and 'My Lord' alternately. Fair shares for all.

'Any order you like, colonel.'

'That's very civil of you, sir. *Any* order,' he mused. 'Let me think.' He paused for a short time.

'I saw Mrs Benson,' he said, 'but that was after the accident. Or was it? Upon my soul, I'm not sure. My Lord,' he added.

'Never mind,' said Andover, 'tell us everything.'

'Everything,' said the colonel, 'I'm afraid that's more than I can remember. Even if I saw it, that is.'

'Tell us everything you can remember.'

'Well, sir, I saw a car and a motor-cycle, and Mrs Benson, and a lot of other people. And the first two collided, my Lord.'

'How long had you seen the first two before they collided, colonel?'

'How long, sir?' queried the colonel. 'How long?' he repeated. 'How would you like the answer, my Lord? In fractions of a minute? Seconds? Or just in general language?'

'Any way you like to begin with, colonel,' said the judge.

'Thank you, sir,' said the colonel. 'I mean my Lord,' he added quickly. His alternate method of answering was landing him in difficulties.

'Would you repeat the question, sir?' said the colonel.

'How long had you seen the car and the motor-cycle before they collided?'

'In general language, sir, a second or two; in fractions of a minute a sixtieth or two; in seconds one or two.'

'And where was the car when you first saw it?'

'Crossing the "halt" line, my Lord.'

'And the motor-cycle?'

'Coming round the bend, sir.'

'Did the car stop at the "halt" line?'

'No, my Lord.'

Andover sat down and Olliphant got up.

'You said your memory wasn't too good, colonel,' he began. 'That's correct, is it?'

'I remember less than I did, sir.'

'And I suppose you may be mistaken in your recollection sometimes?'

'I can't remember having made any mistakes, my Lord.'

'But that could be accounted for by your memory being bad, colonel, couldn't it?'

'If you would point out the mistakes, sir,' said the colonel, 'I would endeavour to correct them. If I remember, that is.'

'D'you often go to the Blue Goose, colonel?'

'Fairly frequently, my Lord.'

'And you usually drink bitter?'

'Most certainly, sir.'

'Mostly in pints?'

'Always in pints, my Lord. I would not insult my swallow with less.'

'Has the Blue Goose any tables outside?'

'No, sir.'

'Then you drink your bitter inside presumably?'

'Of course, my Lord.'

'You wouldn't stand outside flourishing a pint pot?'

'A mug, sir.'

'Very well, then, a mug. You wouldn't stand outside flourishing a pint mug?'

'Flourishing, sir?'

'Holding, then.'

'You have to hold it to drink it, my Lord.'

'Of course, but you don't take it outside to drink in the normal way? It might get knocked, might it not?'

The colonel shivered slightly.

'Yes, indeed, sir.'

'How was it, then, that at the time of the accident you were outside the Blue Goose with a pint pot in your hand?'

'A mug, sir.'

'A mug. How was it that you were outside the Blue Goose with a pint mug in your hand?'

'It was the accident, my Lord.'

'Exactly. But you didn't know there was going to be an accident, did you? You haven't the power of foresight, have you, colonel?'

'Well, I don't know about that, sir. I can tell you a very extraordinary tale of the last war, my Lord.'

'No thank you, colonel,' said the judge hurriedly.

'It was quite extraordinary,' persisted the colonel.

'I dare say,' said Olliphant, 'but his Lordship doesn't want to hear it, nor do the jury.'

'What about you, sir? Would you care to hear it?'

'No thank you,' said Olliphant. 'But you *didn't* know there was going to be an accident, did you?'

'I can't recollect that I did, sir.'

'Then, isn't it a fact that you didn't go outside until you heard a bang?'

'I saw the accident, sir.'

'How can that be if you don't drink your beer in the street, and you didn't know there was going to be an accident?'

'Stranger things have happened to me than that, my Lord, including the episode your Lordship didn't want to hear about.'

'But this wasn't just strange, colonel, it was impossible.'

'Impossible things have happened to me, sir. Well, you'd say they were impossible.'

'Don't worry about the other things,' said Olliphant, 'just explain this one, if you can. If you don't drink your beer in the street, how can you have seen anything before the actual collision?'

'I saw it happen, my Lord.'

'You think you did,' said Olliphant.

'I can agree with you there, sir,' said the colonel. 'I *think* I did, because I *did*.'

'But why should you go into the street with your mug in your hand? What possible reason could there be unless you'd heard a bang?'

'I was there, my Lord.'

'But Mr Olliphant wants to know why,' said the judge.

'I was entitled to be there,' said the colonel.

'So was I,' said Olliphant, 'but I wasn't.'

The colonel, who had been looking rather gloomy, brightened considerably at this statement.

'Then, that accounts for my not seeing you there, sir,' he said.

'Where did you give your statement to the police, colonel?'

'At the police station, my Lord.'

'How did you get there?'

'I walked, sir.'

'Alone?'

'With Mrs Benson, my Lord.'

'And I suppose you discussed the accident together?'

'She is an old lady, sir.'

'I dare say, but she was young enough to walk with you to the station?'

'Yes, my Lord, that is true.'

'And on the way you talked together?'

'We knew each other, my Lord.'

'Exactly,' said Olliphant. 'All the more reason for talking about this horrible accident you'd just both seen.'

'No doubt we discussed it, my Lord.'

'And you were both very angry with the car for not stopping?'

'So would you have been, sir.'

'Quite so. And no doubt you told each other that the car hadn't stopped at the "halt" line?'

'We didn't need to, my Lord, we'd seen it.'

'But you didn't need to tell each other anything, if you'd seen it all. Yet no doubt you did. The car going on, for instance. You talked about hit-and-run drivers, I expect?'

'Indeed, sir, we did. And there he is, my Lord. I'm glad to think he can't hit and run very much from where he is now.'

'How long did it take you and Mrs Benson to walk to the police station, colonel?'

'About ten to fifteen minutes, I should say, my Lord.'

'Did you carry your mug with you?' asked the judge.

'That's a point, my Lord,' said Colonel Brain. 'I can't see myself walking through the streets with a mug. But I can't remember actually putting it down anywhere. I must have, I suppose.'

'Then you must have gone back into the Blue Goose or given it to someone else to take for you?'

'I suppose so, my Lord. If I'd trusted them.'

'Thank you, Colonel Brain,' said Olliphant.

'No re-examination,' said Andover.

'Colonel Brain,' said the judge, 'I found it necessary to fine you £60 for contempt of Court. If I were satisfied that you were not intending to make an exhibition of yourself I might be prepared to remit the fines.'

'Thank you, my Lord. That would be a great help. What with the rates and everything, an extra £60 is quite something to remember.'

'It was meant to be something to remember,' said the judge.

'The Lord Chief Justice never fined me at all,' said the colonel, 'but I still remember him very well.'

'I can't help noticing that, after I'd fined you, you answered questions more satisfactorily.'

'I noticed that too, my Lord,' said the colonel. 'Would it be a good idea, d'you think, to fine every witness? Then you really would get the truth and no mistake. £60 a time! That'd make 'em sit up. "What is your full name and address?" "George Jones of such-and-such." "You're fined £60." You could build new Courts with the proceeds.'

'That will do, thank you, colonel. You may stand down.'

'Thank you, my Lord, and thank you, too, for remitting the fine. It's very good of your Lordship.'

'I haven't remitted it.'

'I could have sworn,' said the colonel, 'that I heard your Lordship say you were prepared to remit the fine.'

'I said I *might* be prepared to remit it.'

'I was never very good at tenses, my Lord, or is it moods?'

'If you go on much longer, colonel, I shall be doubling it and not remitting it. But I'll take a chance and remit both fines this time. But, if you ever have to give evidence again, colonel, kindly remember that evidence is given in a Court of Law not a bar parlour or your own sitting-room.'

'I will, my Lord,' said the colonel, but did not leave the witness-box.

'You may stand down, colonel,' said the judge.

'My Lord,' said the colonel, 'I – I . . . I don't quite know how to put this.'

'What is it?' said the judge.

'I was wondering where I collected the £60 I was fined?'

'You haven't paid it yet.'

'Good gracious,' said the colonel, 'nor I have. That was a narrow squeak. I'm glad you remembered, my Lord.'

'Kindly leave the box.'

The colonel looked round the witness-box as though it had been a room where he had enjoyed a very happy holiday and which he wanted to remember. He took so long in fact that the judge became annoyed and snapped:

'Leave the box, sir!'

The 'sir' made the colonel move. 'As long as they call you colonel,' he told his friends later, 'it's all right. But once they call you "sir" look out for squalls and all that. I can tell you I fairly skipped out of the box. Nearly *fell* out of it. Trod on the foot of the usher. If the judge had heard what *he* said, he'd have sent him down all right. You've got to behave in a Court, you know. Not like a bar parlour or your own sitting-room. That's what the old boy told me. As if I didn't know. But I didn't say so. Not likely. Next time I see an accident I shall turn my back. Nearly cost me sixty quid to see this one. Not worth it. You can buy a TV set for that. But I don't know,' he went on, 'there's a fascination about the Courts. It's the danger, I suppose. The smell of the old gunpowder. Sniping and all that. Put your head up too high or at the wrong moment and bang. You've had it. I nearly called for stretcher-bearers when he added on that fifty quid. Then I'd have been down for the count. But it's like a drug, you know. Once it gets into your blood you're always wanting more. I can't resist it, my dear fellows.' He paused for a moment, trying to recapture his moments in the box. 'There you are, all on your own. They're all gunning for you. Judge, counsel, clerk, usher, policemen, everyone. And you've only got yourself to rely on. Wonderful feeling. How much will they take? You never know. But you must go a bit too far or you'll never get the real fruit flavour. Stands to reason. No danger, no thrill. I'll get six months one day, you know, but it'll be worth it. Or will it? I'm not so sure. That sort of thing is all right till it happens. Then you're sorry. If only I hadn't, you say. But you have. So there you are. No, be sorry first, think afterwards is my motto. Not sure that it sounds right all the same. Still, here we are, and sixty quid to the good. Or not to the bad, at any rate.'

And he stood drinks all round on the strength of it.

Chapter Twelve

Commander Parkhurst

The next witness was Commander Parkhurst, who walked into the witness-box with a pronounced limp but declined to sit down when the judge invited him to do so.

'I'm used to standing, my Lord, thank you,' he said, 'and I shall feel more confidence than if I were sitting down.'

The use of the word 'confidence' made the judge take a quick look at the witness, but he said nothing – except:

'Very well. Let the witness be sworn.'

As soon as this had been done and the necessary formal questions asked, the examination proceeded as follows:

ANDOVER: Now, Commander Parkhurst, I want you to tell my Lord and the jury, in your own words, what you saw at the Blue Goose cross-roads at about 12.30 p.m. on 12 December last.

PARKHURST [*rather fast*]: I was standing outside the Blue Goose public house. I saw the defendant's car approaching the cross-roads from my left. He was coming at a fast speed.

ANDOVER: Don't go too fast yourself please, commander. Just follow his Lordship's pen.

PARKHURST: You asked me to tell the story in my own words, didn't you?

ANDOVER: Yes, commander, but not at your own speed. His Lordship wants to write some of your answers down.

PARKHURST: You'd better ask me questions then. That's the way I talk. I can't alter it just for you. I mean no offence to you, my Lord, but these barristers think they own the place.

JUDGE: Commander Parkhurst, Mr Andover is only trying

to study my convenience, not to irritate you. Perhaps you'd be kind enough to do the same.

PARKHURST: I'll do my best, my Lord, but I'm irritated by a lot of things.

JUDGE: I must remind you that you are not on the quarter-deck now. You are in court, and whatever sailors may think about lawyers, you've got to behave yourself here – like your sailors had to when you were in the Navy. Now don't let's waste any more time. Mr Andover – will you go on, please?

ANDOVER: If your Lordship pleases. Commander Parkhurst, you said you were standing outside the Blue Goose when you saw the defendant's car approach the cross-roads from your left, at a fast speed. What happened next?

PARKHURST: At the same time I saw the motor-cyclist coming along the other road. I could see there would be an accident unless one of them stopped. So ...

ANDOVER: Yes – what happened?

PARKHURST: I was about to tell you. Why d'you have to interrupt me each time? You ask me to tell the story in my own way. Why interfere?

JUDGE: Go on, please, commander, and there's no need to be rude to counsel. He's perfectly polite to you.

PARKHURST: I shouldn't answer his questions at all, my Lord, if he weren't. We still have our rights, my Lord – even a sailor has heard of Magna Charta and Habeas Corpus.

JUDGE: Commander Parkhurst, I'm afraid you may learn a little more about Habeas Corpus if you're not careful, and it will be your corpus which will be involved. If I had not thought that you were, for some reason, in a rather nervy state, I should probably have taken some action against you before.

PARKHURST: I'm not in the least nervy, my Lord. Never felt better in my life. Sailors don't have nerves, my Lord ...

JUDGE: Then pray continue properly with your evidence.

ANDOVER: You said you could see there was going to be an accident. What happened?

PARKHURST: There was one.

ANDOVER: Yes – we know, but tell my Lord and the jury how it happened.

PARKHURST: I have. The two vehicles collided. That's an accident, isn't it?

ANDOVER: Did the car stop at the 'halt' line?

PARKHURST: I've just told you.

ANDOVER: I'm afraid you haven't.

PARKHURST: How could there have been an accident if it had?

JUDGE: Please don't ask questions. You're here to answer them.

ANDOVER: Did the car stop at the 'halt' line?

PARKHURST: Of course not.

ANDOVER: What happened?

PARKHURST: I've certainly told you that.

JUDGE: If I think the question is unfair or repetitive I will say so. Otherwise, commander, you will kindly answer the question. Go on Mr Andover, please.

ANDOVER: You have said the car did not stop at the 'halt' line. What did it do?

PARKHURST: Really! It came on, of course.

ANDOVER: Without stopping?

PARKHURST: Without stopping – or turning round and going back the other way.

JUDGE: Commander Parkhurst, if you're in your senses, you must control yourself.

PARKHURST: It's very difficult, my lord, with such ridiculous questions. A car can only stop or come on. I said it came on. I'm then asked if it stopped.

JUDGE: And did it?

PARKHURST [*sotto voce*]: *Et tu Brute?*

JUDGE: What did he say?

ANDOVER: I didn't catch, my Lord. What did you say, commander?

PARKHURST: I should have said – no, it did not stop. I meant to say – it came on, not stopping. Not having stopped, it came on, not only did it not stop but it came on.

ANDOVER: At what sort of speed?

PARKHURST: It's impossible to judge the speed of an oncoming-not-stopping vehicle.

ANDOVER: But what sort of speed – fast, slow, moderate?

PARKHURST: Fast.

ANDOVER: Did he alter his speed at all?

PARKHURST: Only at the last moment when he braked, but it was too late then.

ANDOVER: What about the motor-cyclist? What sort of speed was he going at?

PARKHURST: Moderate – much slower than the car.

ANDOVER: Then why couldn't he avoid the collision?

PARKHURST: I'd have liked to have seen you avoid it. How can you avoid something which shoots across your path? Unless you've got wings. The motor-cyclist hadn't wings. Nearly got them though, I gather.

ANDOVER: What happened then?

PARKHURST: The motor-cyclist shot over the car and the car drove on. It was a sports car, and *he* was driving it. Why can't they keep them on the racing tracks? They don't care who they kill. All they want is speed.

ANDOVER: Just one other question. Have you known either the accused or the motor-cyclist before or after the accident?

PARKHURST: That's two questions.

JUDGE: It's four as a matter of fact. Kindly answer them all.

PARKHURST: No – no – no – no.

ANDOVER: Thank you, commander. That is all I wish to ask.

JUDGE: Yes, Mr Olliphant, will you start your cross-examination?

OLLIPHANT: If your Lordship pleases. Commander Parkhurst, please don't think that my first question is intended to be offensive, but . . .

PARKHURST: I shouldn't have, if you hadn't said that. Now I shall. That's the way people always start. I don't want to appear inquisitive but –

JUDGE: Be quiet please, commander, and listen to the question.

OLLIPHANT: I repeat, I do not intend to be offensive, commander, but I notice that you're lame.

PARKHURST: You must be remarkably clear-sighted. I've only one leg if you want to know.

OLLIPHANT: I'm extremely sorry, commander. Did you by any chance lose it in a road accident?

PARKHURST: I did not – I lost it in the normal way of duty.

OLLIPHANT: Then I apologize, commander, I didn't know. You seemed to have rather a prejudice against cars and I was seeking for a reason.

PARKHURST: Is that a question?

OLLIPHANT: No.

PARKHURST: Then I take it you don't expect an answer.

OLLIPHANT: Not at the moment, thank you.

PARKHURST: Is that all you wish to ask? Can I go now?

OLLIPHANT: I'm afraid not. I've a good deal more to ask you.

PARKHURST: You'll let me know which are questions and which are statements, won't you?

OLLIPHANT: Certainly, commander. I'm sorry to have upset you so soon.

PARKHURST: You haven't upset me in the least. I'm never upset.

OLLIPHANT: Then you're a very lucky man.

PARKHURST [*bitterly*]: A very lucky man.

OLLIPHANT: I'm sorry, commander, I was not referring to your leg.

PARKHURST: Nor was I. I can manage very well without a leg. You only thought I was lame, didn't you?

OLLIPHANT: Commander, you seem to be extremely bitter about something. It's not your leg. What is it?

PARKHURST: Have I got to answer that?

JUDGE: Unless it has something to do with the accident, I don't see why you should.

PARKHURST: It has nothing to do with the accident. And bitter is not the right word.

OLLIPHANT: Very well, commander, let me come to the accident. What were you thinking about at the time?

PARKHURST: How do I know?

OLLIPHANT: Well, you weren't thinking about the accident?

PARKHURST: Of course not. It hadn't happened.

OLLIPHANT: You weren't thinking about the traffic?

PARKHURST: I've no idea what I was thinking about.

OLLIPHANT: Let me see if I can help you.

PARKHURST: I don't need any help, thank you. I don't know and that's that.

OLLIPHANT: Would you agree, commander, that you're not one of those exceptional people who can think of two things at the same time?

PARKHURST: I'm not an exceptional person at all.

OLLIPHANT: And you can't think of two things at the same time?

PARKHURST: Of course not. One at a time's enough for me.

OLLIPHANT: Well, if you weren't thinking about the traffic what were you thinking about?

PARKHURST: That's a question, isn't it?

OLLIPHANT: And what's the answer? Perhaps we'd better start a bit earlier. What time did you get up that morning?

ANDOVER: Really, my Lord, is this relevant?

OLLIPHANT: It is highly relevant, my Lord. The witness has given detailed evidence of how the accident happened. I am going to submit in due course that, unless he was watching the vehicles, he in fact saw nothing except perhaps the collision. I shall submit that he has reconstructed the incident as he thinks it happened – quite honestly, of course. If he was thinking about something else at the time, he couldn't have seen what he says he saw.

JUDGE: I don't think I can stop that line of inquiry, Mr Olliphant. I must rely on you not to carry it too far.

OLLIPHANT: Thank you, my Lord. Now, tell me, commander, do you remember getting up that morning?

PARKHURST: I do.

OLLIPHANT: Did anything particular happen that morning?

PARKHURST: No, nothing particular.

OLLIPHANT: Will you be good enough to tell my Lord and the jury as far as you remember, exactly what happened that morning from the time you got up until the time of the accident?

PARKHURST: Have I got to do that, my Lord?

JUDGE: I'm afraid so, yes.

PARKHURST: It will be very embarrassing to me, my Lord.

JUDGE: It's very embarrassing to the accused to be charged with a serious offence.

PARKHURST: And I have to tell the whole truth?

JUDGE: You have sworn to do so.

Reluctantly the commander started to state what had happened.

'Do you want it from the beginning?' he asked.

'Yes, please,' said Olliphant.

'Well, my wife called me at eight o'clock or thereabouts with a cup of tea. She said breakfast would be in half an hour. I thanked her and said I'd be down in time. What on earth this has to do with the accident I do not know.'

Olliphant said nothing.

'D'you want me to go on?'

'Yes, please.'

'In detail?'

'Yes, please.'

'Very well,' said the commander, but he paused some time before he went on – so long that the judge said:

'Well, commander?'

'I'm thinking how to put it, my Lord. It's not easy.'

'Just say what happened, commander.'

'I then had a conversation with my son. D'you want to know what I said?'

'Yes, please, commander,' said Olliphant.

'You would,' said the commander, but too quietly for the judge to hear. 'Very well,' he went on. 'I said to Johnny something like this. "Good morning, Johnny. It's a lovely day again. What are we going to do today? Bit of fishing, d'you think? Or just a walk? Perhaps you're right. We want a bit of exercise. At least I do. You haven't got a paunch yet – I should hope not, at fifteen. It is fifteen, isn't it? Last Thursday week. You had a happy birthday, didn't you? Here – where's my leg? Are you sitting on it? You've not hidden it again? That's not playing fair." I then called down to my wife and asked her if I'd left my leg downstairs. She looked for it, said I had and that she'd bring it. Then I spoke to my son again and said how kind his mother was but that she didn't quite understand about us, about our secret. Then my wife came up with my leg. I dressed, came down to breakfast. I said that I was going for a walk and she said that lunch would be at one. I said I'd be back in time. Haven't you had enough yet?'

'You're doing very nicely, commander, thank you,' said Olliphant. 'Please go on.'

'You don't know what *you're* doing,' said the commander.

'Please go on,' repeated Olliphant.

'I then took my son for a walk across the fields. I suggested to him that we should wind up at the Blue Goose and have a drink. On the way I said to my son that there was something I wanted to talk to him about. "D'you really want to go into the Navy?" I asked him. "You don't have to, just because I did. It's not what it was, either. Orders were orders in my day. Didn't have to put everything into triplicate and have questions asked in the House if you used your initiative. If you'd prefer something else you've only got to say. Only we ought to make a decision fairly soon, or it'll be a bit late. You see, there's a lot to learn whatever you go in for. And now's the time, when your mind's supple. Old chaps like me have brains like steel – we can't understand anything unless it's drilled home. But you're quick. By Jove you are. What have you ever thought of? I don't mind a bit. It's your life. If it's music you want, you shall have it – if you want to be a long-haired painter, I don't mind – or a short-haired one either, who paints houses. It's your life, Johnny, it's your life." Well, I'm not sure what else I said. We walked in silence for some time. Then I looked at my watch and saw that I'd be missing my half-pint if I didn't increase the pace. So we stepped it up a bit. I can manage quite well. We got to the Blue Goose and I remember saying to my son: "Well, now for a quick half-pint and then home. In we go. They won't notice your age – you look sixteen anyway." We went into the pub and I ordered my drink. After a few minutes we left. As we walked away from the Blue Goose I said to Johnny: "Now, have you made up your mind? Really it doesn't *have* to be the Navy – anything you say" – and I meant it, my Lord – anything he said, anything.' The commander paused and then said:

'And that's the lot as far as I remember.'

'You mean,' said Olliphant, 'that it was then that the accident happened?'

'Yes,' said the commander.

'It sounds a very one-sided conversation with your son,' said Olliphant. 'Just before the accident didn't he have anything to say?'

'It was an entirely one-sided conversation,' said the commander. 'My son lives here,' – he tapped his head. 'Or rather, here,' and he put his hand over his heart.

Olliphant paused for a moment and then he asked:

'How old was he when he died?'

'Three.'

'I'm sorry to have to ask you this, commander, but how did he come to die?'

The commander paused. Then he looked into space and said harshly:

'One of your flaming sports cars got him.'

'I'm very sorry, commander,' said Olliphant. 'That's all I wish to ask.'

'No re-examination,' said Andover quickly, and Commander Parkhurst limped out of the witness-box.

Chapter Thirteen

Patricia

The next witness was Miss Patricia Gaye, or at any rate that is the name by which the usher called her. She was an attractive girl of twenty-two, inclined to be pert, full of confidence and looking forward to going into the witness-box. This was going to be a new experience indeed. Up to date her most important thrills were acquired by being cuddled by boy friends, but, although she still looked forward to thrills of the same kind, this was a very different affair. Indeed, she looked forward to recounting it to her boy friends between the thrills.

She had enjoyed to some extent the proceedings before the magistrates, but had decided not to show off there. After all, there was no judge in robes, only a bench of ordinary people in ordinary clothes. Even counsel looked ordinary without wig and gown. But the Old Bailey was a very different proposition. She had read about it so often. Mostly grim tales of murderers, but some others too. And now she herself was going there – not as a visitor, queueing up for a place in the gallery, but as a witness, with the right to sit in the body of the Court when she had given her evidence. She was glad she was called early in the proceedings, as it would give her the chance of seeing most of the trial. Yes, it was going to be a great day, and she dressed for the part.

Before she was sworn the clerk asked her to state her full name.

'That's rather a question,' she replied. 'You see, I have several full names.'

'What name are you generally known by?' asked the clerk.

'Most people just call me Pat.'

'The clerk wants to know your ordinary names, christian names and surname,' said the judge.

'Well, you see, it depends,' began Patricia.

'What were you born?' asked the judge.

'Alice Drewe.'

'Well, as you're not married, that's your name,' said the judge. 'Let's get on, please. Kindly take the oath.'

Andover had been chatting to Olliphant during this conversation, and only half-heard what was said. As soon as she had been sworn, he looked at the proof of her evidence in front of him, and said:

'Is your full name Patricia Gaye, and do you live at 12 Peppercorn Road, Sandy Lane?'

'Well, the judge says it isn't,' said Patricia.

'I'm so sorry,' said Andover, 'it was my fault. Is your full name Alice Drewe?'

The examination and cross-examination of Patricia then went on as follows:

PATRICIA: Well – you see, it isn't really.

JUDGE: I thought you said you were born Alice Drewe.

PATRICIA: I was, my Lord, but I changed it.

JUDGE: To what?

PATRICIA: D'you mean the first time?

JUDGE: Have you changed your name several times then?

PATRICIA: Well, my Lord, in a way – yes.

JUDGE: Why?

PATRICIA: The first time, my Lord?

JUDGE: How many times were there?

PATRICIA: Well, my Lord, it all depends what you mean by changing my name.

JUDGE: What d'you mean?

PATRICIA: What do I mean by changing my name?

JUDGE: Yes.

PATRICIA: Changing my name.

JUDGE: So do I.

PATRICIA: Thank you, my Lord.

JUDGE: Mr Andover, we haven't got very far yet. What is this lady's name?

ANDOVER: My Lord, I had it as Patricia Gaye.

PATRICIA: That's right.

ANDOVER: Then that's your name.

PATRICIA: Well, it was, but I'm not sure that I'm keeping it on.

JUDGE: Really, Mr Andover, it's the duty of the Prosecution to know the names of its own witnesses.

ANDOVER: I'm sorry, my Lord. I didn't know of the complications. When did you change your name from Alice Drewe?

PATRICIA: Well – I didn't exactly.

ANDOVER: But you just said you did.

PATRICIA: Well, of course I did change it, but it wasn't me exactly who did it. It was my parents.

JUDGE: Then let's get on. Your parents were Mr and Mrs Drewe, and they changed their name to Gaye.

PATRICIA: Very well, my Lord.

JUDGE: But that's right, isn't it?

PATRICIA: No, my Lord.

JUDGE: Your parents' name was Drewe?

PATRICIA: Yes, my Lord.

JUDGE: And they had a child called Alice – and that was you?

PATRICIA: Yes, my Lord.

JUDGE: And then they changed their name to Gaye?

PATRICIA: No, my Lord, they changed it to Wagstaffe.

JUDGE: Did they change it again after that?

PATRICIA: No, my Lord.

JUDGE: So you are the daughter of Mr and Mrs Wagstaffe?

PATRICIA: Yes, my Lord.

JUDGE: And you were christened Alice? Then you're Alice Wagstaffe.

PATRICIA: I see, my Lord.

JUDGE: But THAT IS YOUR NAME, isn't it? It is correct that you're not married isn't it?

PATRICIA: Well – yes – I mean no, my Lord, not yet.

ANDOVER: Very well, Miss Gaye. Is your full name Alice Wagstaffe?

PATRICIA: Well – I'm terribly sorry – but I've sworn to tell the truth, and it isn't.

ANDOVER: What are you usually known by?

PATRICIA: I told you – Pat.

ANDOVER: That's among your friends and relatives. What would strangers call you?

PATRICIA: I don't speak to strangers.

JUDGE: Mr Andover, I've had enough of this. Will you and the witness kindly make up your minds what her name is and then the trial can proceed.

ANDOVER: If your Lordship pleases. Will you agree to Patricia Gaye for today, at any rate, Miss Wagstaffe?

PATRICIA: It's the name I use for modelling.

ANDOVER: I dare say.

PATRICIA: I use Moira Allen for photographs.

ANDOVER: No doubt.

PATRICIA: I was Wagstaffe at school.

ANDOVER: That will do about the name, Miss Gaye.

PATRICIA: Of course, when Mother remarried I changed the Wagstaffe with her.

ANDOVER: Will you please forget about the name, Miss Gaye.

PATRICIA: I wasn't exactly adopted – not officially, that is. But I changed my name with Mother.

ANDOVER: Very well then.

PATRICIA: It was to Hardcastle, as a matter of fact.

ANDOVER: Miss Hardcastle – I mean Miss Gaye – did you . . .

PATRICIA: So they're five really. Drewe, Wagstaffe, Hardcastle, Gaye and Allen. That's why I get muddled.

JUDGE [sternly]: Miss Gaye . . .

PATRICIA: It sounds rather bad, having all those names – until you know the reason.

JUDGE: Miss Gaye, will you kindly stop talking, and let counsel ask you a question.

PATRICIA: I'm sorry, my Lord. I'm new here.

ANDOVER: Now, Miss – Miss – Miss [sotto voce] confound

it ... anyway – did you witness an accident by the Blue Goose cross-roads on the 12th December last?

PATRICIA: I don't remember the date. I never was any good at them.

ANDOVER: Well, you've only seen one accident recently – and that's the one we're talking about. You can take it from me it was on the 12th December.

PATRICIA: I don't remember.

ANDOVER: I dare say you don't remember the date – but you remember the accident?

PATRICIA: Oh yes – but not the date. It was terrible. I had to turn my head away.

ANDOVER: But you saw what happened before you turned your head away?

PATRICIA: Oh yes – as clear as I can see you.

ANDOVER: Then just tell my Lord and the jury what you saw.

PATRICIA: I saw the accident.

ANDOVER: Yes – but we want the details ... how it happened –

PATRICIA: I thought you knew.

ANDOVER: Never mind what we know. We want to know what you saw.

PATRICIA: Well, I saw him flying over the car and then I turned my head away.

ANDOVER: Yes – but what did you see before you saw him flying over the car?

PATRICIA: I saw it all.

ANDOVER: Then tell us about it. Start from the beginning.

PATRICIA: The beginning of what?

ANDOVER: Of what you saw.

PATRICIA: I told you.

ANDOVER: You told me you saw the whole thing. What was the whole thing?

PATRICIA: The accident.

ANDOVER: Did you see anything before you saw the man flying over the car?

PATRICIA: I told you – I saw it all. But I had to turn my head away then.

ANDOVER: No doubt. But before then?

PATRICIA: Perhaps it was silly of me, but I hate blood. I was frightened.

ANDOVER: I don't want to know anything about that part of the accident. Who was the accident between?

PATRICIA: The two of them of course.

ANDOVER: The motor-cyclist and the car, you mean?

OLLIPHANT: Please don't lead the witness.

ANDOVER: There's no dispute that the two collided.

OLLIPHANT: I dare say, but I shall be obliged if you won't lead this witness.

ANDOVER: When did you first see either of the two of them?

PATRICIA: Either of the two of them?

ANDOVER: Either of the two vehicles which collided.

PATRICIA: I saw them coming along.

ANDOVER: Where from?

PATRICIA: I've no idea. I didn't know either of the drivers.

ANDOVER: No – I mean on which road was each coming along?

PATRICIA: Well – the car was coming from my right and the motor-cyclist from in front of me.

ANDOVER: Do you know these cross-roads?

PATRICIA: Oh yes – very well.

ANDOVER: Then you know the 'halt' sign in the road the car was coming along?

PATRICIA: I should say. I once didn't stop on my bicycle. And there was a policeman. But he was ever so nice about it.

ANDOVER: So you know the 'halt' sign well.

PATRICIA: I met him at a dance later, and we had a good laugh about it.

ANDOVER: No doubt – but ...

PATRICIA: No ill feelings, I hope – he said ...

ANDOVER: Never mind about the policeman.

PATRICIA: He's a sergeant now.

ANDOVER: When you first saw the car, where was it?

PATRICIA: Coming along the road.

ANDOVER: Did it stop at the 'halt' line?

PATRICIA: Oh no – it just came straight on.

ANDOVER: How fast?

PATRICIA: Like a racing car. It just whizzed by.

ANDOVER: Did it not stop at all?

PATRICIA: Well, it just stopped for the motor-cycle to hit it and then it went on again.

ANDOVER: How fast was the motor-cycle going?

PATRICIA: Oh – quite slow. He was a nice-looking boy. I had to turn my head away.

ANDOVER: Well, we're all very glad that he's quite all right now.

PATRICIA: To look at him, no one would know anything had happened to him.

ANDOVER: Then you know him?

PATRICIA: Oh – I just met him outside.

JUDGE: I thought you didn't speak to strangers, Miss ... Miss Gaye?

PATRICIA: Well – my Lord, we all felt rather matey outside. It's like being in a boat together – or a railway carriage – or a coach – or a bus ... on a long journey, of course – or ...

JUDGE: Never mind, Miss Gaye. Yes, Mr Andover?

ANDOVER: That is all I wish to ask.

JUDGE: Yes, Mr Olliphant?

OLLIPHANT: Miss Gaye, you were standing on the side of the road opposite the Blue Goose?

PATRICIA: Yes – I always wait there. It doesn't look well, standing outside a public house. At least Mother always says that. It lowers you.

OLLIPHANT: Quite so. You were waiting for someone I suppose?

PATRICIA: Well – yes.

OLLIPHANT: May I ask who?

PATRICIA: I'm not sure.

OLLIPHANT: Well, really, Miss Gaye, I'm quite certain a young lady like you would know whom you were meeting.

PATRICIA: Well – I should have.

OLLIPHANT: I'm afraid I shall have to ask you a bit more about this, Miss Gaye. But please don't think I'm trying to pry into your private affairs.

PATRICIA: Oh – that's quite all right. They weren't any of them serious – not to say serious.

OLLIPHANT: What I want to put to you, Miss Gaye, is that you saw nothing of the accident at all – until you heard a bang, looked up and saw the motor-cyclist going over the car. And then you turned your head away. That's right, isn't it?

PATRICIA: I turned my head away all right. So would you, I shouldn't be surprised.

OLLIPHANT: But the rest is right too, isn't it? You were thinking about the person whom you weren't quite sure you were meeting, and not thinking about motor-cars or accidents, were you?

PATRICIA: I wasn't thinking of anything – I don't think, really. Not just then, I wasn't. I was waiting.

OLLIPHANT: Well, let's see about that. What time did you leave home that morning?

PATRICIA: About eleven, I think, but I can't be sure.

OLLIPHANT: Well – tell me what happened that morning before you left home.

PATRICIA: What happened?

OLLIPHANT: Yes – from the time you got up.

PATRICIA: Everything?

OLLIPHANT: Yes, please.

PATRICIA: Oh – very well.

OLLIPHANT: Yes, Miss Gaye. What time did you get up?

PATRICIA: About half past eight. I ought to explain. I had a bath the night before.

OLLIPHANT: Quite so.

'Well,' Patricia went on, 'the first thing that happened was that Mum asked me what time I came in the night before. "What time did you come in last night?" she said. You know the way mums do. I said I didn't know. I expect you did that when you were a young man.'

'Don't speak to counsel like that,' said the judge.

'I'm sorry, my Lord,' said Patricia. She drew a breath and went on:

'Well, Mum didn't quite believe me. So I said we'd had a puncture. We hadn't, as a matter of fact.'

'So you were prepared to lie to your mother?' said Olliphant.

'Of course,' said Patricia. 'Everyone does.'

'What did your mother say?'

'She asked me who I'd been with, and I said, "Simon, of course." And she said, "Why of course?" and I said, "Well, he was with me." Then mother said I hadn't seen much of him recently, and I said that Simon was all right for a time but that I wasn't all that keen. That was true.'

'What about the puncture?' asked Olliphant.

'Oh – it was only two o'clock when we got home. Not all that late. Simon's all right, you know. For a time, that is. He was ever so sweet that night, as a matter of fact. Now, where was I? Oh, yes. Just then Mum remembered that there was a message for me. When I asked from whom, she said, "from George." And I was thrilled. Really thrilled. I've got quite a thing about George. "What did he want, Mum?" I asked her. She said he wanted me to meet him. Of course I asked where, and Mum wasn't very pleased. She said he'd asked me to meet him outside the Blue Goose, but that he'd rung off before she could tell him she didn't like me meeting boys in the street. It cheapens me, she said. Well, I think that if you are cheap it doesn't matter where you meet a boy, in the Ritz or whatever. And if you aren't cheap, you won't seem cheap wherever you meet him. Anyway, Mum made me promise that I wouldn't stand outside the pub itself but on the other side of the road. And I promised. I kept it, too.'

'Don't you always?'

'Didn't you ever have a mother?' asked Patricia.

'Now, Miss – Miss ... ' the judge fumbled for the name and said something quite unintelligible in place of her name. 'I've told you once before not to speak to counsel like that.'

'I'm sorry, my Lord,' said Patricia. 'But it did seem so

silly asking if I always kept promises. Well,' she went on, and drew another breath, 'well, I was just thinking how lovely it was going to be to see George, but I suddenly thought of something. "He did say George Bennett, Mum, didn't he?" I said. "He just said George," said Mum. "But, Mum, you must remember," I said. "It might have been George Oatley." Mum remembered him. She liked him better than the other. Well, George O. was nice, but I was feeling like George B. at the time. "George Oatley gave you that nice brooch for Christmas," said Mum. "I like him." "George B. gave me a nicer," I said. It wasn't really nicer, but I told you, I was feeling like George B. at the time. "What time did he say, Mum?" I asked. "Twelve thirty." "But do try and think which of them it was," I said. But Mum couldn't. "It might have been either," she said. "You'll know sure enough when you see him." "But which brooch will I wear, Mum?" I said. And she said to take them both, to put one on and change it if it was the wrong George. She's a good sort, Mum, really. I bet she knew a thing or two when she was a girl.'

'What happened after that?' asked Olliphant.

'Well, I went to the Blue Goose and waited. Not on the same side. I told you I'd promised not to. And, as I was waiting, Tony came along and asked me to have a cup of coffee with him. Of course I said I couldn't. Because I was waiting for George, you see. But I didn't say it was George. I just said someone. You don't want everyone to know your business, do you? Though Tony's quite a nice boy. At Christmas time and such like. Not as a regular. All right under the mistletoe. Well – you know what I mean. Of course that made him want to know more than ever. "Ask no questions and you'll hear no lies," I said. "Must be someone important," he said. "You're all tarted up." I don't like expressions like that, and let him know it with a few of my own. "Sorry," he said. "I only meant you looked particularly inviting." "Well, I'm not inviting you," I said. "Nice brooch you've got," he said. I must say Tony knows when to change the subject. "Which d'you like better?" I said, and brought out the other. "Why d'you wear one and carry the other?" he asked. That gave me an idea. "Thanks, Tony," I said. " 'Bye." He took the hint and went off, and I started to put the other brooch on, and then it happened.'

'Well, Miss Gaye,' said Olliphant, 'you were still wondering which George it was going to be, weren't you?'

'I suppose I was.'

'So you couldn't have noticed much about cars and motor-cycles, while you were thinking of an important thing like that, could you?'

'I couldn't help seeing the accident,' said Patricia.

'You couldn't help *hearing* it, and you looked up and saw the man going over the car. That's all you really do know, isn't it?'

'I think I saw the car coming along.'

'Of course you do,' said Olliphant. 'That's because everyone talked about it afterwards, isn't it? They were all very angry with the car driver, weren't they?'

'Well,' said Patricia, 'he didn't stop.'

'Of course. And you just heard what everyone said and believed you'd seen it. That's it, isn't it?' said Olliphant.

'Well,' replied Patricia, 'it's quite a time ago now, isn't it?'

'Of course it is. Thank you, Miss Gaye. That is all I wish to ask.'

'No re-examination,' said Andover.

'And which George was it, Miss Gaye?' asked the judge.

'Must I answer that?' said Patricia.

'Not if you'd rather not,' said the judge.

'Oh – well,' said Patricia. 'In for a penny in for a pound. He didn't show up.'

'I'm sorry,' said the judge.

'Oh, it's all right,' said Patricia. 'On the way back from the police station I met a friend.'

Chapter Fourteen

Mr Berryman

The next witness was Esmond Stuart, who had been in a car following the motor-cycle. He was asked to say what happened.

STUART: Well – I was coming along the road behind a motor-cycle ...

ANDOVER: What sort of speed?

STUART: D'you mean me or him?

ANDOVER: Both of you.

STUART: Well, I was catching him up. So I suppose he was going about forty and I was doing about fifty. It's not restricted.

ANDOVER: And what happened?

STUART: Well, I came round the bend and slowed a bit for the cross-roads and then suddenly I saw there was going to be an accident ahead of me. So I jammed on my brakes.

ANDOVER: You couldn't give any idea of how the accident happened?

STUART: Only that the motor-cyclist ran into the car. It all happened in a flash.

ANDOVER: Thank you, Mr Stuart. No, don't go. Mr Olliphant may want to ask you something.

OLLIPHANT: Tell me, Mr Stuart, how near were you to having a collision of your own?

STUART: Not what I should call near. I stopped five feet short of the motor-cycle.

OLLIPHANT: You stood on your brakes, I imagine.

STUART: So do I. To tell you the truth I can't actually

remember braking. But, as I stopped, I must have. The thing was all over in a moment.

OLLIPHANT: I expect your brakes screamed, didn't they?

STUART: I shouldn't be at all surprised, but I can't really say I remember hearing them.

OLLIPHANT: Can you say whether you had stopped before the motor-cyclist went over the top of the car – or after?

STUART: About the same time I should think, but it's all rather guess-work. I certainly saw him go over the top. It's a nasty sight and I can remember seeing it, but I was concentrating on stopping, I imagine.

OLLIPHANT: Thank you, Mr Stuart.

ANDOVER: So you were looking at something and thinking about something else at the same time.

STUART: I don't follow.

ANDOVER: Never mind, Mr Stuart. I was just testing my learned friend's theory on you.

OLLIPHANT: It's not a theory at all. Of course a man who's driving can think about driving and what's on the road at the same time. He's got to. It's all part of the same operation. What I say is that it's physically impossible for an ordinary person to think which brooch she's going to wear and at the same time to record in her mind the paths of a car and a motor-cycle which don't concern her.

JUDGE: I think we'd better leave these matters until you are addressing the jury, Mr Olliphant.

OLLIPHANT: If your Lordship pleases.

After Mr Stuart had given evidence, the driver of the motor-cycle was called but, as Andover had stated, he remembered nothing of the accident. So his evidence only took a few minutes. He was only called by the prosecution in case Olliphant wished to cross-examine him and to avoid the suggestion that he was being kept out of the witness-box. As he did not even remember that he had used his motor-cycle that day, he added nothing to the evidence already given.

The next witness called by the Crown was Arnold Berryman, and his examination and cross-examination proceeded as follows:

ANDOVER: Now, Mr Berryman, will you tell my Lord and the jury exactly what you saw, please.

BERRYMAN: Well, I was walking past the Blue Goose on the other side of the road, when I saw the car and the motor-cycle coming towards each other, and they collided.

ANDOVER: Did the car stop at any time before the collision?

BERRYMAN: Neither before nor after the collision.

ANDOVER: What about the motor-cyclist?

BERRYMAN: He couldn't help himself. The car came in front of him, and he couldn't avoid it.

ANDOVER: What sort of speed was the car travelling at?

BERRYMAN: I'm no judge of speed, but fast.

ANDOVER: And the motor-cyclist?

BERRYMAN: Slower than the car.

ANDOVER: Thank you, Mr Berryman.

JUDGE: Yes, Mr Olliphant?

OLLIPHANT: Mr Berryman, were you just going for a walk – or were you going to some particular place?

BERRYMAN: I was going for a walk.

OLLIPHANT: You were walking towards the car?

BERRYMAN: That's right.

OLLIPHANT: What did you do after the accident?

BERRYMAN: I stopped and ran to the assistance of the motor-cyclist.

OLLIPHANT: So until the actual collision you continued walking?

BERRYMAN: That's right, as far as I remember.

OLLIPHANT: Do you say that you actually followed the path of the car and saw that it did not stop at the 'halt' line?

BERRYMAN: Yes, I do.

OLLIPHANT: You weren't interested in the car at all, were you?

BERRYMAN: No – I can't say I was.

OLLIPHANT: Are you sure you followed its course?

BERRYMAN: Yes.

OLLIPHANT: And it was coming fast?

BERRYMAN: Yes.

OLLIPHANT: So that from the time you first saw it until the collision was only a matter of a second or two?

BERRYMAN: I suppose so.

OLLIPHANT: Then will you tell me how you were able to see the motor-cycle before it was almost on to the car?

BERRYMAN: I saw it. That's all I can say. I was there and I saw it.

OLLIPHANT: How far away was it when you first saw it?

BERRYMAN: Twenty to thirty yards, I suppose.

OLLIPHANT: But you haven't got eyes in the side of your head. If you were watching the car, how on earth could you have seen the motor-cycle until they were on each other?

BERRYMAN: I can switch my eyes or my head very quickly. I expect I did so.

OLLIPHANT: But you couldn't watch both the car and the motor-cycle at the same time.

BERRYMAN: Not at exactly the same split second of time, but I can turn my eyes from one to the other.

OLLIPHANT: Well, if you did that you must have seen that there was going to be a collision.

BERRYMAN: I did.

OLLIPHANT: You haven't said that before.

BERRYMAN: I wasn't asked.

OLLIPHANT: Anyway, that's what you say now. You definitely saw there was going to be a collision?

BERRYMAN: Yes.

OLLIPHANT: Then why didn't you stop?

BERRYMAN: I did.

OLLIPHANT: Not until after the actual collision.

BERRYMAN: Well – I may have stopped before.

OLLIPHANT: You may have done anything, Mr Berryman, but your actual words were these: Question – What did you do after the accident? Answer – I stopped and ran to the assistance of the motor-cyclist.

BERRYMAN: Well, I may have stopped before then.

OLLIPHANT: If you'd seen that there was likely to be a collision it would give you a shock.

BERRYMAN: It did.

OLLIPHANT: I suggest that was only at the moment of impact. That before then you just continued on your stroll. If you'd seen there was going to be a crash, you'd have stopped dead, wouldn't you?

BERRYMAN: I did.

OLLIPHANT: But not until after the accident.

BERRYMAN: I've told you I may have been wrong about that.

OLLIPHANT: At any rate you've no recollection of suddenly stopping in your tracks because you could see two vehicles – about twenty yards or so away from each other – about to collide?

BERRYMAN: I can't say exactly. It was all over very quickly. I can only say that I've come here to tell the truth and that's what I've told you.

OLLIPHANT: I'm sure you mean to, Mr Berryman.

BERRYMAN: I've no interest in sending another man to prison – even if he didn't stop after the accident.

OLLIPHANT: But you must have thought that was a pretty bad thing to do?

BERRYMAN: Who wouldn't?

OLLIPHANT: I quite agree. Now, Mr Berryman, another matter. You were going for a stroll before lunch. To give you an appetite, I suppose?

BERRYMAN: I was going for a stroll – that's all I can say.

OLLIPHANT: And had you anything particularly on your mind that day?

BERRYMAN: Not that I can remember.

OLLIPHANT: As you passed the Blue Goose, did you perhaps wonder whether to cross the road and have a drink before lunch?

BERRYMAN: I don't drink.

OLLIPHANT: Or buy some cigarettes?

BERRYMAN: I don't smoke.

OLLIPHANT: What are your hobbies, Mr Berryman?

BERRYMAN: I do a bit of gardening. I don't know if you'd call that a hobby.

OLLIPHANT: Certainly. Anything else? D'you read at all ... listen to music?

BERRYMAN: I read a certain amount.

OLLIPHANT: What sort of books?

BERRYMAN: Mostly history books.

OLLIPHANT: No fiction – crime stories, or that sort of thing?

BERRYMAN: No.

OLLIPHANT: What were you reading at the time of the accident?

BERRYMAN: I wasn't reading. I was walking.

OLLIPHANT: No – I mean what book were you in the middle of at home?

BERRYMAN: I don't remember that. It may have been a book about Queen Elizabeth.

OLLIPHANT: Did you find it interesting?

BERRYMAN: Very.

OLLIPHANT: D'you think you might have been thinking about it while you were walking?

BERRYMAN: Quite possibly.

OLLIPHANT: You don't remember, I suppose, what you were thinking about just before you saw the accident?

BERRYMAN: I've no idea.

OLLIPHANT: I suppose you have some problems in your life – even minor ones to do with your garden.

BERRYMAN: Nothing serious.

OLLIPHANT: But you may have been thinking about your garden?

BERRYMAN: Quite possibly.

OLLIPHANT: Or the book about Queen Elizabeth?

BERRYMAN: Yes – I may have been.

OLLIPHANT: Do you usually think about something when you go for a stroll?

BERRYMAN: I expect so. It's difficult to have a blank mind.

OLLIPHANT: You're concentrating now upon answering my questions, aren't you?

BERRYMAN: I'm trying to.

OLLIPHANT: Could you think about your garden at the same time?

BERRYMAN: Think what about it?

OLLIPHANT: Think anything about it. Think what you're going to grow next year – instead of the things which didn't come off. Think if you want to have a rockery at the end of the garden, and so on. Could you think about any of those things and answer my questions carefully at the same time?

BERRYMAN: I shouldn't think so. D'you want me to try?

OLLIPHANT: No, thank you. Finally let me ask you this. D'you suppose you could think about Queen Elizabeth or your garden or anything else like that, and at the same time follow the course of two vehicles coming at right angles to each other at the same time?

BERRYMAN: Well, I did.

OLLIPHANT: You think you did.

BERRYMAN: Of course I think I did, because I did.

Chapter Fifteen

Mr Piper

Mr Piper came next. He gave much the same evidence as the other witnesses had given in examination-in-chief. He was quite definite that the car had not stopped at the 'halt' line. At the end of his examination by Andover, he said:

'Can I now be a-going of?'

'Not yet,' said Andover, 'Mr Olliphant will want to ask you some questions.'

'Which is Mr Olliphant?' asked Mr Piper.

'I am,' said Olliphant, who was already on his feet.

Mr Piper smiled pleasantly at him, as though to say 'how d'you do?' but did not in fact speak.

Olliphant then began:

OLLIPHANT: Mr Piper, your story is just the same as that of the other witnesses, isn't it?

PIPER: That all a-goes for to show how true it is.

OLLIPHANT: Or that you are all wrong.

PIPER: I am not to be a-taken as agreeing to that.

OLLIPHANT: Then we'll try to find something we can agree upon. Tell me, Mr Piper, what were you doing at the time of the accident?

PIPER: I was a-taking of the air.

OLLIPHANT: Is the air outside the Blue Goose particularly good?

PIPER: Are you a-sinuating that I am a-partial to the smell of beer? Because if so you are a-right.

OLLIPHANT: Then we're agreed. Before we've finished probably we shall be agreed about everything.

PIPER: I shouldn't be too a-sure of that.

OLLIPHANT: That's all right, Mr Piper. We'll take it by stages.

PIPER: That's a-right. More a-haste less a-speed.

OLLIPHANT: Precisely. Many a mickle makes a muckle, if you'll forgive me.

PIPER: Least a-said, soonest a-mended.

JUDGE: Mr Olliphant, I take it you'll come to the accident some time?

OLLIPHANT: I'll a-try, my Lord. Now, Mr Piper, you were taking the air outside the Blue Goose. May I take it that you had previously taken the air inside it?

PIPER: Not only the air, I'm a-glad to be saying of.

OLLIPHANT: And how much of the other stuff had you a-taken of?

PIPER: Do you wish an exact answer?

OLLIPHANT: More or less.

PIPER: Because I keep a record here of my consumption.

OLLIPHANT: Why?

PIPER: At the end of each year I add it up and divide by the number of days in the year, three-sixty-five or three-sixty-six as the case may be.

OLLIPHANT: And what, may I ask, is the object of that?

PIPER: The same as with a car. I like to be a-knowing of what the rate is.

OLLIPHANT: Then if it's too high you cut it down?

PIPER: I would not be a-saying of that. But you may say that if it is too low I bring it up.

OLLIPHANT: And how is it at the moment?

PIPER: I have not prepared figures up-to-date but I would say that it was a little under average. But my birthday is a-coming.

OLLÍPHANT: Quite. And what is the approximate average per day?

PIPER: May I write it down, my Lord?

JUDGE: Why?

PIPER: I would not want to be a-showing off, my Lord.

JUDGE: How much beer d'you drink a day?

PIPER: It is more impressive by the year, my Lord.

Between two thousand and two thousand five hundred a year.

OLLIPHANT: Two thousand what? Gallons?

PIPER: Alas no. I can only claim pints.

OLLIPHANT: Then you have six or seven pints a day?

PIPER: Except when I'm a-staying of in the hospital.

OLLIPHANT: What d'you go to hospital for?

PIPER: When I'm a-breaking of my leg.

OLLIPHANT: How often does that happen?

PIPER: When I'm a-falling down of.

OLLIPHANT: And how often do you fall down? Does it depend on the number of pints?

PIPER: That is an offensive but accurate a-way of putting it.

OLLIPHANT: Is your consumption spread over the day?

PIPER: It is. It keeps me a-smiling of all day.

OLLIPHANT: And were you then a-smiling of at the time of the accident?

PIPER: I'm always a-smiling of when I'm a-taking of the air.

OLLIPHANT: And how would you describe your smile? A five-pint smile, d'you think?

PIPER: More like half-a-gallon.

OLLIPHANT: We won't quarrel about a pint.

PIPER: No one could quarrel about a pint. It isn't made for quarrelling of.

OLLIPHANT: Quite so. And how long did you go on smiling?

PIPER: Until the accident.

OLLIPHANT: And then what did you do?

PIPER: I saw that there was helpers enough for the injured man, so I started a-repairing of the damage to myself.

OLLIPHANT: What damage?

PIPER: The smile had been a-taken off my face.

OLLIPHANT: So you went back to the Blue Goose to restore it?

PIPER: I was a-shaking of at the legs.

OLLIPHANT: Exactly. And when did you make your statement to the police?

PIPER: After I'd come out again.

OLLIPHANT: Were you quite fit again?

PIPER: I would not be a-saying I was fit, but I was a-smiling again.

OLLIPHANT: Another half-gallon smile?

PIPER: I must be a-looking of that up.

OLLIPHANT: Never mind.

PIPER: I have it here. Ah – I have a-found it – three pints less.

OLLIPHANT: Less! What does that mean?

PIPER: Some was spilled.

OLLIPHANT: So when you made your statement to the police you'd had eight pints of beer and you were smiling?

PIPER: Eight pints less.

OLLIPHANT: Very well, less.

PIPER: One wants to be accurate in these places.

OLLIPHANT: And do you think that in that condition you really remembered what you'd seen – if indeed you'd seen anything?

PIPER: Well, I should have. We'd a-been a-talking of nothing else.

OLLIPHANT: So you'd had three pints' worth of talk about the accident?

PIPER: Three pints – less.

OLLIPHANT: All right – three pints less. But everyone had been talking about the accident?

PIPER: Naturally we got a-piecing of it all together.

OLLIPHANT: And what you've told us today is the result of what you pieced together with your friends in the bar of the Blue Goose?

PIPER: It was all done most carefully.

OLLIPHANT: I'm sure – except that someone jogged your arm apparently.

PIPER: Not at all. It was while I was still a-shaking of.

OLLIPHANT: Thank you, Mr Piper. That's all I wish to ask you.

ANDOVER: Thank you, Mr Piper.

PIPER: Have I got to be a-going now? I was just beginning to be a-liking of it here.

Chapter Sixteen

Joan

Then Joan Anderson came into the witness-box. She had given evidence to the same effect as the other witnesses in the Magistrates' Court. After she had been sworn, Andover asked her where she was at the time of the accident, and what she saw.

'I was walking past the Blue Goose when I saw the accident,' she said.

'When did you first see the car?' asked Andover.

'Before it got to the cross-roads.'

'Did it halt at the "halt" line?'

'Yes.'

'Miss Anderson,' said Andover, 'I asked you if it halted at the "halt" line.'

'And she said "yes",' said Olliphant.

ANDOVER: Mr Olliphant, will you kindly not interrupt. I want to be sure that the witness understood the question. Miss Anderson, did you understand the question?

JOAN: I think so.

ANDOVER: What was it?

JOAN: You asked me if the car halted at the 'halt' line.

ANDOVER: What car do you think I am referring to?

JOAN: The one that was hit by the motor-cycle.

ANDOVER: That's right. Now, did you see the car before it reached the 'halt' line?

JOAN: Yes.

ANDOVER: Now – don't answer in a hurry. Think carefully first. Did it stop at the 'halt' line?

JOAN: I think it did.

ANDOVER: You think it did?

JOAN: Yes.

ANDOVER: Do you remember giving evidence at the Magistrates' Court?

JOAN: Yes.

ANDOVER: Did you think it did then?

JOAN: I don't remember.

ANDOVER: My Lord, in view of the depositions, I ask leave to treat this witness as a hostile witness.

JUDGE: She doesn't give the impression of being hostile, but in view of the depositions, you may.

ANDOVER: Miss Anderson, do you know the accused?

JOAN: No, sir.

ANDOVER: Do you know the motor-cyclist?

JOAN: No.

ANDOVER: Have you ever spoken to either of them?

JOAN: No.

ANDOVER: Or to their solicitors?

JOAN: No.

ANDOVER: You remember giving evidence before the magistrates in the other Court, some weeks ago?

JOAN: Yes.

ANDOVER: You seem to have changed your mind about the accident since then.

JOAN: Have I?

ANDOVER: Did you not say at the Magistrates' Court that the car never stopped at the 'halt' line – but came on fast?

JOAN: I may have done.

ANDOVER: May she see her deposition, please. Is that your signature?

JOAN: Yes.

ANDOVER: Well – which is right? What you said then, or what you say now?

JOAN: What I say now.

ANDOVER: Why?

JOAN: Because it is, that's all. I must have made a mistake before.

Andover sat down.

JUDGE: Any questions, Mr Olliphant?

OLLIPHANT: No, my Lord.

JUDGE: Don't you want to ask her what she may have been thinking about?

OLLIPHANT: No, thank you, my Lord.

JUDGE: Or what she was doing at the time?

OLLIPHANT: No, thank you very much, my Lord.

JUDGE: Or why she changed her mind about what happened?

OLLIPHANT: No, thank you very much indeed, my Lord.

JUDGE: Well, I think I shall. Miss Anderson, what were you thinking about at the time of the accident?

JOAN: Do I have to say that?

JUDGE: I'm afraid so.

JOAN: My baby, my Lord.

JUDGE: I see. What about your baby?

JOAN: It was going to be adopted, my Lord.

JUDGE: And has it been adopted?

JOAN: No, my Lord.

JUDGE: Why not?

JOAN: Because I want it. I love it, my Lord.

JUDGE: Then why was it going to be adopted?

JOAN: Because my parents wanted me to.

JUDGE: But you didn't?

JOAN: No, my Lord.

JUDGE: Then what were you thinking about at the time of the accident?

JOAN: I was so unhappy, my Lord.

JUDGE: Where were you going?

JOAN: I was going with the paper to have it signed.

JUDGE: You mean you were on your way to have your consent witnessed by a magistrate?

JOAN: Yes, my Lord.

JUDGE: But you didn't want to consent?

JOAN: No, my Lord.

JUDGE: But you had decided to give in to your parents?

JOAN: I'd nowhere to keep it.

JUDGE: And your parents wouldn't have it at home?

JOAN: No, my Lord. They said it was a disgrace, my Lord,

and they didn't want it advertised. I didn't think it a disgrace, my Lord. I'm proud of it. And it's not like giving up a doll or a puppy. A baby's different, my Lord. And it was all mine, my Lord.

JUDGE: Now don't start getting distressed. I gather you're going to keep the baby?

JOAN: Yes, my Lord.

JUDGE: How are you going to manage?

JOAN: I've got a job, my Lord, and I've found a place where the landlady says she loves babies, and she'll look after it in the day and ... and ...

JUDGE: Well – that's good. But what else were you going to say?

JOAN: And I've got a young man, my Lord, and he says we may keep it when we're married, my Lord.

JUDGE: Well, that's all very satisfying. How did all this come to happen? You were on your way to sign the paper when the accident happened.

JOAN: Yes, my Lord.

JUDGE: What happened after the accident?

JOAN: Well – after I'd given my statement to the police a lady asked some of us in to her house and gave us a cup of tea. And then I decided I wouldn't sign the paper, my Lord. And the lady we had tea with told me of someone who might help me.

JUDGE: So it really comes to this – that if it hadn't been for the accident you might have lost your baby?

JOAN: Yes, my Lord.

JUDGE: You must have felt very grateful to the accused for having had the accident, Miss Anderson. Very, very grateful.

Joan did not say anything.

'But why did you say, at the Magistrates' Court, that the car *didn't* stop at the "halt" line?' the judge went on.

'I hadn't had time to think about it, my Lord.'

'And now you've had too much,' commented the judge. 'Tell me,' he went on, 'at the time you gave your evidence at the Magistrates' Court you hadn't met the young man who's offered to marry you?'

'Yes, my Lord, I'd met him.'

'But he hadn't offered to marry you?'

'No, my Lord.'

'It comes to this, doesn't it, that at the time of the hearing before the magistrates you were glad that you were going to keep your baby but it was going to be difficult for you?'

'Yes, my Lord.'

'You were happier than when the baby was going to be adopted, but not so happy as you are now?'

'No, my Lord.'

'You're very happy now?'

'Oh, yes, my Lord, very happy.'

'So you want everyone else to be happy?'

'Yes, my Lord.'

'I expect you're very glad the motor-cyclist has recovered?'

'Very, my Lord.'

'And I don't suppose you'd like to see Mr Barnes convicted?'

'No, I wouldn't, my Lord.'

'D'you think that can have anything to do with your changing your evidence, Miss Anderson?'

'I've had more time to think, my Lord. The car *did* stop, I'm sure.'

'Very well,' said the judge. 'Thank you.'

Chapter Seventeen

Mr Salter Again

Mr Salter, the retired schoolmaster, was the last witness. He gave his evidence-in-chief in much the same way as he had done in the Magistrates' Court. After Olliphant had elicited from him in cross-examination that the car was going fast, the motor-cyclist was going at a very moderate speed, and that he couldn't be sure if the latter could have avoided the accident by braking, he went on:

'Mr Salter, you wanted some cigarettes just before the accident?'

'Yes.'

'You were just going to buy them?'

'Yes.'

'What make were you going to buy?'

'Cosmopolitan, I think.'

'What kind of Cosmopolitan?'

'I'm not sure. *Crown*, I think.'

'How many?'

'Twenty-five or fifty.'

'Hadn't you made up your mind?'

'I don't remember.'

'But I should imagine, if I may say so, from the deliberate way in which you have given your evidence, that you are a man of decision.'

'That may be your opinion.'

'Is it a fact?'

'What has this got to do with the case, may I ask?'

'If the learned judge thinks I shouldn't ask the question, he will say so. Otherwise, kindly answer it. Are you not a man of decision?'

'I can make up my mind.'

'And usually do?'

'Often.'

'But sometimes, like everyone else, you have to weigh-up the various considerations affecting the decision before you make it?'

'You can put it that way.'

'But that's right as far as you are concerned?'

'I suppose so.'

'How do you normally buy your cigarettes?'

'Really, my Lord,' said Mr Salter, turning to the judge, 'have I got to answer these ridiculous questions?'

'Yes,' said the judge, 'and they are not ridiculous.'

'How do you normally buy your cigarettes?' repeated Olliphant.

'It varies.'

'Sometimes twenty-five, sometimes fifty, some times a hundred?'

'Yes.'

'Which is the more usual?'

'It varies. Fifty or twenty-five, I should say.'

'D'you usually make up your mind before you go into a shop, or when you're inside?'

'That varies too.'

'Usually before?'

'Possibly.'

'What about this occasion? Had you made up your mind how many you were going to buy?'

'I can't say. I may have done.'

'Had you made up your mind as to the kind of Cosmopolitans you were going to buy?'

'I expect so.'

'How long before the accident did you decide you wanted some cigarettes?'

'Not long.'

'But had you gone out specially to buy some, or did you suddenly think you'd like to get some?'

'I hadn't gone out specially to buy them.'

'You'd gone for a stroll?'

'Yes.'

'And just before the accident you decided you wanted some cigarettes?'

'Yes.'

'Now, you were a schoolmaster, Mr Salter, and no doubt you have considered from time to time how the mind works?'

'Well?'

'Once you had decided you wanted cigarettes your mind had to deal with the question of what brand and what type and how many?'

'I suppose so. But I knew the brand. I never smoke any other.'

'But the type varied?'

'Yes.'

'Well, can you remember if your mind had yet gone through that process, when the accident happened?'

'No, I can't.'

'Would it be correct to say that normally before you walk into a shop you've got your object cut and dried?'

'Usually, yes.'

'So, immediately before the accident you must have been saying to yourself, "shall it be twenty-five or fifty? Shall it be Crown or some other variety?" That's so, isn't it?'

'It may have been so.'

'So you weren't concentrating on looking at the traffic?'

'Not concentrating – no.'

'Which did you see first, the car or the motor-cycle?'

'I can't say.'

'Are you sure of that?'

'Sure that I can't say? Yes, I am.'

'Well, if you can't say which you saw first, you can't have seen the car cross the "halt" line.'

'I did.'

'If the prosecution's witnesses are right, the car was coming faster than the motor-cycle, so that if you saw the motor-cycle come round the bend you can't have seen the car at the "halt" line.'

'Then I must have seen the car first.'

'Are you sure of that?'

'No, but you say it must be so and I'll accept that.'

'When did the driver of the car first cause you anxiety? When you saw the motor-cycle?'

'I suppose so.'

'Because you realized there'd be a collision?'

'Yes.'

'You know these cross-roads well, don't you?'

'Yes.'

'There were a lot of accidents until they put up a "halt" sign?'

'This one was after.'

'I didn't ask you that. You knew they were dangerous cross-roads?'

'Yes.'

'And when you saw both vehicles, you knew there was going to be another accident?'

'Yes.'

'And then you naturally became alarmed?'

'Naturally.'

'Why weren't you alarmed before, when you saw the car cross the "halt" line?'

'If, as you say, I must have seen it first, I couldn't at that moment tell there was anything else on the road.'

'No, but there might have been. There was in fact.'

'Yes.'

'And you knew the danger. Here was a car charging across the "halt" line and it didn't worry you till you saw the motor-cyclist?'

'I didn't say it was charging across.'

'You're quite right. Someone else said that. Well, how did it go across. Fast, I thought you said?'

'Yes.'

'Well, what's the difference between "going across fast" and "charging across"?'

'Charging across suggests a reckless disregard for other people's safety.'

'And isn't that what *you* meant when you said he came fast across?'

'I meant what I said.'

'I dare say you did. If a car goes across a "halt" line into the junction of two roads, at a fast speed, hasn't the driver of the car a reckless disregard for other people's safety?'

'Before now you've told me that my opinion was irrelevant.'

'Now I'm asking you your opinion. Has not the driver of a car driven in the way I've described a reckless disregard for other people's safety?'

'Your client nearly killed a man.'

'Then the answer is "yes"?'

Mr Salter hesitated. He knew what would follow if he said 'yes', and had, therefore, endeavoured to avoid saying it. He knew that he had quibbled when he pretended to distinguish between charging across a road and going fast across it, but he very much disliked the idea of being given the treatment he had often handed out to boys at school. His own flair for cross-examination, when it was partially sadistic, made him like even less the same treatment handed out to him, though he knew there was nothing sadistic about Olliphant's questions. It was just inexorable logic. He cursed himself for having yielded to the temptation of trying to side-step Olliphant's question – 'Here was a car charging across the "halt" line and it didn't worry you until you saw the motor-cyclist?' He knew what the next question would have been if he had said it had not worried him. So, like many a foolish schoolboy, he had tried to avoid the consequences by a stupid quibble. He ought to have known better.

'The answer is "yes"?' persisted Olliphant.

'I'd like to modify a previous answer,' said Mr Salter.

He realized as he said it that this effort to extricate himself from an impossible position might make things even worse for him. This was not school, where *he* could call a halt when he liked. It was not a game where there was a timekeeper and he might be saved by the gong. Olliphant was a very skilful professional cross-examiner, and he wasn't going to let go, and Mr Salter knew it.

'By all means in due course,' said Olliphant pleasantly. 'But first of all would you kindly answer my question, and possibly one or two more.'

'Would you mind repeating it?'

All the tricks – or, rather, fumblings – of the discredited witness, but Mr Salter couldn't think of anything else to do. If he'd been at home writing an essay on the subject, he might have thought of better answers to make, but here he was in the witness-box, with everyone waiting for his answer. And the silences while he tried to wriggle out of Olliphant's grasp were almost as intolerable as the questions themselves.

'Certainly,' said Olliphant. 'It is quite a time since I asked the question. What I asked was whether a driver who drove fast across cross-roads, ignoring a "halt" sign, was not, in your opinion, guilty of a reckless disregard for the safety of other people?'

'I thought you phrased the question rather differently.'

Mr Salter was now in it for better or worse, and though he knew that it was idle to postpone the evil moment, like a hunted animal he was now desperate and determined to try anything. But his case was worse than that of a hunted animal. A thunderstorm, a gate, a bog, another animal, a host of things may intervene to save it. But Mr Salter was doomed and he knew it, and his struggles merely made his destruction even more certain, if possible, and even more unpleasant. He could recognize all the signs, even though he was not experienced in the Law Courts. Olliphant had always been a courteous and quiet cross-examiner, seldom raising his voice, never even appearing to lose his temper, never adopting a bullying manner, always letting the witness say what he wished without interruption. But now he was becoming even more pleasant. His bedside manner was even more obvious. His patience was even more pronounced. Lesser men would have jumped on the witness for the quibble, and jumped on him with a show of indignation. That, of course, would have had *some* effect, but far less. To begin with, once counsel starts being stern with a witness the sympathy of a Court or jury is likely to turn in favour of the witness. But Olliphant saw to it that it was the other way round. Some at least of the jury would see the quibble and be indignant about it themselves. To them Olliphant would appear the kindest possible person who, though constantly insulted by the witness, took not the slightest offence. Moreover, by not putting an end to the quibble by one short, sharp show of indignation, Olliphant was leading him on and on to quibble and prevaricate to a horrible degree. But once he had started, he felt he had to go on.

'You're perfectly right, Mr Salter,' said Olliphant smoothly. 'The effect of my question was exactly the same, but I didn't use precisely the same language. Though I don't mind which question you answer – the one of which you apparently recollected the phraseology or the one I've just asked.'

'I didn't say I recollected the phraseology. I said it sounded different, and it did.'

'My fault entirely,' said Olliphant, 'but perhaps you wouldn't mind answering the question as I've put it now – if you remember it.'

Olliphant was paying out the rope to an unexpected extent. He didn't really believe that Mr Salter would fall for the last four words, but he thought he would just give him the chance.

Mr Salter looked at Olliphant. Both men knew exactly what was happening. Olliphant was saying in unspoken, words: 'My dear fellow, if you really enjoy tying yourself up, I'll go on handing out the rope as long as you like.' Mr Salter was not asking for mercy but, for the first time in his life, as far as he could remember, he felt like doing so. He despised such behaviour. He had always remembered a boy whom he was about to punish.

'Couldn't you overlook it this time, sir?' the boy had asked.

'Overlook it?' he had answered, and paused. He remembered the pause too. It was not on his conscience because, if you are made like that, you behave like that and don't reproach yourself with it. But he had always remembered the look on the boy's face during the pause. After it had gone on long enough he had repeated: 'Overlook it?' and added, 'No, I'm afraid not.'

As Mr Salter looked at Olliphant he actually wondered whether to ask for mercy, but he soon realized that it was not in Olliphant's or the judge's power to release him from the vice in which, with Olliphant's assistance, he had pinned himself. All he could do was to submit to the inevitable. But now there was a further danger. Mr Salter had taken an oath to tell the truth, and he knew very well that this wriggling on his part was not a proper compliance with that oath. He had not committed perjury but there was always a risk that, if he struggled too hard to extricate himself from his position, he might in an unguarded moment say something which could be proved to be untrue. Mr Salter could not know that not only are prosecutions for perjury extremely rare but that it was almost impossible that a witness with no interest in a case should be prosecuted, even if he did in a misguided moment say something which he knew to be untrue.

Mr Salter's look became one of resignation and, though in his heart there was the trace of fear, he did not allow this to appear on his face.

'Yes, please,' he said eventually. 'I'd be glad if you'd repeat it.'

'I hope your pupils had better memories than you, Mr Salter,' said the judge.

'The young do have better memories than the old,' replied Mr Salter.

He was still able to bite a finger, if someone put it near enough. He saw by the look on the judge's face that he had scored. Only a small point, but not bad to score from the position in which he was. *And* over the judge. He was emboldened to have another snap, and he added:

'And I believe, my Lord, that the witness-box is not the best place to test a memory.'

'Are the jury to gather from that,' asked the judge, 'that

they must not pay too much attention to your evidence as you find giving evidence too much of a strain on your memory?'

'I think the witness-box must be a strain for anyone, my Lord,' said Mr Salter, 'even though he is an entirely independent witness who has volunteered a statement in the public interest and has no wish to be subjected to hours of questioning by counsel and by your Lordship.'

Another point for Mr Salter. The judge recognized the justice of his answer and said no more. But he still had Olliphant to deal with, and Olliphant was waiting patiently for him.

'Certainly I'll repeat it,' he said. 'You must forgive me,' he added, 'if once again I put it slightly differently. But there will be no difference in the sense. In your view, Mr Salter, would it be a reckless disregard of the safety of other people for a driver to disregard the "halt" sign at the Blue Goose cross-roads and endeavour to go straight across them at a fast speed?'

There was no escape this time, and Mr Salter almost welcomed the fact.

'Yes,' he said.

'Now, I believe you wanted to modify one of your previous answers,' went on Olliphant. 'By all means do so.'

Mr Salter had by this time forgotten that belated attempt to admit his earlier blunder. Suddenly being given the opportunity he was quite unable to take advantage of Olliphant's offer.

'I've forgotten for the moment what it was,' he said.

'Then by all means let me know when you've remembered,' said Olliphant. 'Meanwhile, perhaps you'd tell me this. You now agree that the car was being driven with a reckless disregard for the safety of others. Why didn't that worry you until you actually saw the motor-cyclist?'

Mr Salter remembered now. That was the question he had wanted to avoid.

'I remember now what it was I wanted to modify. I was wrong to say that it didn't worry me when I saw the car being driven as you say.'

'Was that a slip of the tongue or a mistake of memory, then?'

'It might have been either.'

'You mean that? It might have been either?'

Confound! thought Mr Salter. He's got something waiting for me if I say I do mean it. I thought it better to have both excuses available. Apparently it'll be worse. But which shall I abandon? I've simply no idea.

'Well, Mr Salter, did you mean what you said. That it might have been either – slip of the tongue or a fault in your memory?'

'I thought you said a mistake of memory.'

He himself could hardly tell why he insisted on this futile parrying of a question.

'Your memory is improving,' said the judge.

'I'm as surprised as your Lordship,' said Mr Salter.

'Was it mistaken memory or a slip of the tongue?' persisted Olliphant.

'It was a mistake,' said Mr Salter, 'though whether of the tongue or memory I couldn't at this stage say.'

'But, if it had been a slip of the tongue, surely you would have corrected it before, Mr Salter? If you really remember the car crossing the "halt" line, and if you weren't really considering what cigarettes to buy, if you're really talking of something you actually can remember seeing, then you must equally well remember the shock it must have given you to see the car driven in this disgraceful manner, irrespective of the motor-cyclist altogether? Do you?'

'That was a very long question. Do I what?'

'Do you remember the shock you received when you first saw the car?'

'I can't say that I actually remember a shock.'

'Why not? You've just taken the trouble to correct an answer you made. You now say that you were wrong to say that you weren't worried when you first saw the car. What worried you?'

'The way the car was being driven.'

'Have you ever seen a car driven like that before?'

'Not to my knowledge.'

'Then surely it was a shock?'

'I suppose it must have been.'

'But you've just said you don't remember it.'

'No.'

'Apparently you remember being worried but not being shocked. Is that it?'

'It could be.'

'What, in your opinion, is the difference between worry and shock in these particular circumstances?'

Mr Salter said nothing.

'Is there any difference?'

'Perhaps not.'

'So you *do* remember being shocked?'

'I suppose I do.'

'Before you saw the motor-cycle?'

'I suppose so.'

'But a moment ago you said you couldn't remember being shocked.'

'Did I say that?'

'You did indeed. Now just think, Mr Salter. Cast your mind back to your stroll on the day of the accident.'

'Yes?'

'Try and remember your walking along and deciding you wanted some cigarettes.'

'Yes.'

'Isn't it a fact that the next thing you knew was that there was a collision?'

'It was very close.'

'It was while you were still thinking how many or what cigarettes to buy?'

'It may have been.'

'I suggest it was the collision which took your mind off the cigarettes, and nothing else.'

Mr Salter again remained silent.

'Will you swear that that was not the case?'

'How can I be sure at this distance of time?' asked Mr Salter.

'That is all I wish to ask,' said Olliphant, and sat down.

'Only two questions,' said Andover. 'Did you, or did you not, see the car before it crossed the "halt" line?'

'I saw it.'

'Did it stop at the line, or not?'

'It did not.'

Chapter Eighteen

Speeches

'Well,' said Andrew, as he and Michael left the Court, 'what did I tell you? Olliphant has fairly chopped up those prosecution witnesses so that even their own solicitors wouldn't recognize them.'

'He was first rate,' said Michael. 'A wonderful performance. I can't say how grateful I am to Wimbledon for suggesting him.'

'It's in the bag,' said Andrew. 'Once the jury hear your evidence they'll sling the case out. Bet you five to one they don't retire.'

'There's only one snag,' said Michael.

'There isn't *any* snag,' replied Andrew. 'Juries don't like convicting in motoring cases anyway, but this is a piece of cake.'

'Still, there *is* a snag. You said that, once the jury hear my evidence, they'll sling out the case.'

'Well?'

'They're not going to hear my evidence.'

There was a moment or two of silence. Andrew couldn't believe what he'd heard and said so.

'I'm not going to give evidence,' said Michael.

'Why on earth not?'

'Never mind why.'

'But you must be mad. Or have you been leading us up the garden and the car didn't stop at the "halt" line after all?'

'I would stake my most solemn oath that it did.'

'That's all you're asked to do. Why on earth won't you?'

'Because I won't, that's all.'

Andrew thought hard for nearly a minute.

'Is there another woman?' he asked.

'Another woman!' said Michael. 'Now it's you who are talking drivel.'

'Is there one?'

'Of course not.'

'Would you swear to that too?'

'Certainly. What on earth put the idea into your head?'

'Quite simple,' said Andrew. 'This most effective method of cross-examination by Olliphant *could* be adopted by the other side. *You* could be asked what *you* were thinking of just before the accident. So, if you were thinking about Millicent or Belle or Felicity, you'd have to say so, unless you were prepared to commit perjury.'

'I see,' said Michael. 'I certainly wouldn't commit perjury, but there isn't another woman. And I'm not giving evidence. That's final.'

'Olliphant will be livid. He'll think you've been lying to him.'

'I can't help what he thinks.'

'He might throw up the case.'

'D'you really think he would?'

'I don't know, but it's conceivable, I suppose. You've assured him that the car stopped and he's cross-examined a dozen witnesses merely to show they're wrong, and then you won't *swear* that it did stop.'

'We'd better go and see him, I suppose.'

'I should jolly well think so. Soon as we can. If you've got to get someone else you won't have a lot of time. It won't look well, anyway. And, of course, you *do* realize that you may be convicted if you don't go into the box?'

'I see the danger, but I'm still not going in. I suppose counsel for the Crown will make a great deal of it.'

'As a matter of fact *he* can't. He's not allowed to comment on your failing to give evidence.'

'Good. I didn't know that.'

'But the judge can comment on it. And Olliphant himself – or whoever your counsel is – will have to refer to it. He can't pretend to ignore it. It'll stand out a mile. The one person who doesn't give evidence is the driver.'

'Well, there it is. We must do the best we can. I suppose I'd better ring Wimbledon and get him to arrange a conference with Olliphant.'

'At once. And tell him why. So that they know what they've got to deal with.'

Very early next morning Michael and Andrew met Wimbledon outside Olliphant's chambers and were soon shown in to him.

'Now, what *is* all this?' asked Olliphant. 'Why are you not prepared to give evidence?'

'I'm afraid I can't tell you that,' said Michael, 'but I assure you that it isn't because the car didn't stop at the "halt" line. It did.'

'Mr Barnes,' said Olliphant, 'you're a public man and, if I may say so, of great ability. You must know what you're doing. You've told me that, apart from the political aspect of the matter, the outcome of this case is of vital importance to your wife's health. I should be failing in my duty to you if I did not say two things – first, although I seldom am rash enough to state the probable outcome of a criminal trial, in the circumstances of this case I am going to tell you that if you give evidence – even only moderately well – you are bound to be acquitted. *Bound* to be acquitted, I say. If you don't give evidence, you may be convicted.'

'But I *may* still be acquitted?'

'Oh, yes,' said Olliphant. 'It is possible that the unsatisfactory nature of the evidence for the prosecution may lead the jury to acquit you – even if you don't give evidence. But they'll want to know *why* you don't give evidence. And they may draw the inference that the reason you don't is because you can't swear truthfully that you stopped at the "halt" line. No one could blame them for taking that view.'

'Mr Olliphant,' said Andrew. 'Might I make a suggestion?'

'Of course.'

'I need hardly say that I agree with everything you've said. Before we came here I said much the same – though not, of course, as well or as forcibly. If you'll forgive my saying so, it occurs to me as possible that the very weapon you used so very skilfully and effectively against most of the witnesses might be used on Michael, with disastrous effect.'

'How d'you mean?'

'Now, I believe Michael to be a most truthful person. Suppose he is asked what he was thinking about just before the accident, and suppose the truth is that he was thinking about a highly-confidential matter relating to politics or personal relationships?'

'Then he could say so.'

'But you probed much deeper than that. You insisted on being told what the exact matters were. Couldn't prosecuting counsel do the same?'

'He might. How far he was allowed to go would depend on the judge.'

'Well, then, if you can't assure Michael that he won't be asked about what occurred just before the accident, may he not be frightened of the possible repercussions of such questions being asked? For example – he has assured me that he is not having an illicit love affair – and I believe him – but suppose he had been, and had been thinking about the other girl. He'd either have to commit perjury, or admit it. Where would he be then?'

'Is that the reason, Mr Barnes?' asked Olliphant.

'I'm sorry,' said Michael, 'I can only say two things – first that the car did stop at the "halt" line and secondly that I'm not going into the witness-box to say so.'

'Well, Mr Wimbledon, what d'you think?' asked Olliphant.

'I'm utterly astounded,' said Wimbledon. 'I must confess I've been wondering if you and I ought to retire from the case.'

'Certainly, if the client would like us to do so,' said Olliphant.

'By no means,' said Michael. 'That's the last thing I want. I'll be most grateful if you'll remain.'

Olliphant thought for a moment. Then:

'I don't think we're entitled to retire,' he said. 'Our client still assures us that the car stopped. And he has never promised us that he would be giving evidence – we have just assumed it as a matter of course. A person charged with a crime is under no duty whatever to give evidence. It's only a little over sixty years since he was first *permitted* to do so. It's a privilege, not a duty. I can find no way in which Mr Barnes has misled us. Naturally, his refusal to give evidence may shake your or my belief in the justice of his case. But our beliefs are of no importance, and indeed may be quite wrong. No, as far as I am concerned, I'm perfectly prepared to go on appearing for you, Mr Barnes, much as I regret and fail to understand your behaviour. But I must ask you just once. Is your decision quite final? If it is, I shall have to prepare a different speech for the jury, and I don't want to find that at the last moment you change your mind. Though, as a matter of fact, I should be very pleased if you did. Even though it meant scrapping my final speech. Your evidence would be worth more than a thousand speeches of mine.'

'No, I shan't change my mind,' said Michael. 'My decision is absolutely final.'

'Very well, then,' said Olliphant. 'I've told you the possible consequences and it'll be your responsibility, not mine, if you go down.'

'I understand that,' said Michael.

Two hours later, when the concluding stages of the trial had been reached, Michael was full of admiration for the almost nonchalant way in which Olliphant announced that he called no evidence. It might have been the obvious thing to do from the way he said it. He said the words as though they were a pure formality, indeed as though that was what everyone expected him to say. The judge was extremely surprised, but did not disclose the fact. Counsel for the prosecution gave Olliphant a slightly startled look.

'You go first, old boy,' Olliphant said quietly to him, in the same, almost lazy, way in which he had made the announcement about not calling Michael.

Andover was certainly taken aback. He had expected to be able to cross-examine Michael and he had realized that, unless he made a substantial inroad into his evidence, the jury were going to acquit. Although it is no part of prosecuting counsel's duty to try to secure a conviction at all costs, he would not be human if he did not normally wish the prosecution to succeed. As an advocate, it is difficult for him to feel otherwise. In a sense Andover's task was now easier, but it was not all that easy, as Andrew was right in saying that *he* was not allowed to comment on the defendant's failure to give evidence.

'May it please your Lordship, members of the jury,' he began, 'you have now heard all the evidence in this case, and the question you have to consider is whether the evidence as a whole convinces you that the accused is guilty. His Lordship will direct you upon all matters of law, and anything I say will be subject to what his Lordship may tell you. In a way this case is more simple than many accident cases, because you may think, as appears to be conceded by the accused's learned counsel, that everything depends upon whether the accused stopped at the "halt" line or not. If he did stop there, I should not ask you to convict him of this charge, and vice versa. Now, members of the jury, you have heard altogether eight witnesses, all of whom were at one time sure that the car did *not* stop. It is perfectly true that my learned and ingenious friend has, by his skilful cross-examination, cast doubts upon the reliability of some of these witnesses. It is also true that one of the witnesses changed her story and said that the car *did* stop. But, in view of the circumstances in which she came to change her story, you may not attach much importance to her evidence either way.

'Now, Mr Stuart does not really help you as to how the accident happened. Colonel Brain, you may think, never saw the accident at all. And let me say this, members of the jury, if you have a doubt about the reliability of any witness, by all means disregard his or her evidence. But, when you have gone through that refining process, what remains? You have the definite evidence of Mr Salter and of Mr Berryman, and, to a lesser extent, that of Mrs Benson. Why should these witnesses – who know neither the accused nor the injured man – be so sure that the car never stopped at the "halt" line, if it did? No one suggests that any of them has a grievance against the accused, or that they are not seeking to tell you the truth. So that the only real issue is whether they are reliable in their observation and recollection.

'Why should they all make a mistake, members of the jury? And the same mistake. Why? I suggest to you that there is no reason whatever why they should. There was the "halt" line, members of the jury. There was the car. You may well ask yourselves how can a person like Mr Berryman or Mr Salter solemnly swear that the car crossed the "halt" line without stopping if they weren't looking in that direction and saw the incident. Where is the room for mistake? We can, of course, all make mistakes and in many accident cases it is very difficult to tell where the truth lies. But, in this case, members of the jury, with the one exception, which I suggest you disregard, with that one exception everyone said the car came across the line without stopping. And these two witnesses, Mr Salter and Mr Berryman, I suggest to you are people of responsibility, normal, ordinary, solid people such as yourselves. I do not intend to be offensive either to Colonel Brain or Mr Piper when I concede that you might hesitate to rely on their evidence. Still less do I intend to be offensive to the unfortunate Commander Parkhurst whose evidence I concede might – only might, mind you – be coloured by the tragic loss of his son. Miss Gaye also you may possibly think a trifle too – too – and again I do not mean to be offensive to the young lady – a trifle too flighty, a trifle too engaged upon her interest in boy friends – to be a reliable witness.

'You will, I hope, notice, members of the jury, that I am not seeking to rely upon any piece of evidence which might for any reason be considered suspect. It is no part of my duty to press for a verdict of guilty. It *is* my duty, however, to draw your attention to what I may call the solid evidence in the case. And it is upon the evidence as a whole that you have sworn to try this case. Any piece of evidence which you consider might be unreliable by all means disregard. Take Mrs Benson, for instance. She is an elderly lady and, for that reason alone, you might hesitate to accept her evidence without reserve. Some people see and think at eighty-two as well as much younger people, but it is not generally the case and you do not know Mrs Benson sufficiently to be sure of her physical and mental capacity. Moreover she might, it is true, have been concentrating more on the recovery of her own licence than of what was happening round about her. Nevertheless, you are entitled to give some weight to her evidence, if you think fit, particularly if it is the same as that of solid reliable witnesses.

'So once again I come back to Mr Salter and Mr Berryman. Both sensible, ordinary people. Both certain they saw what happened. Both certain the car did not stop at the "halt" line. If you doubt whether they are right in their observation and recollection – that is an end of the matter. But where is there room for doubt? It is perfectly true that my learned friend in his cross-examination of Mr Salter put him in the sort of difficulty in which you may think any honest man trying to remember what happened might be put. But at the end of it all, what did he say? "The car did not stop at the 'halt' line." I suggest that upon this evidence there is no doubt in this case and that, unpleasant as your duty must be, I submit to you that the prosecution has proved its case with the certainty which is required by law, as his Lordship will tell you.

'There is a further point, members of the jury. No one has suggested that the police in this case have in any way been unfair. How is it, then, that every single witness says the same thing, or said it immediately after the accident? If there had been one person to say the opposite, either his name would have been given to the accused to enable him to call him for the defence, or I myself would have called him. But there is no one, members of the jury. No one. Everyone who has given evidence, with the one exception, has told you the same story. What reasonable doubt can you have but that it happened as they have sworn?'

Andover sat down and Olliphant began his final speech. After a short preliminary, he went on: 'Members of the jury, there was once a well-known Lord Chief Justice of England who was a profound thinker. In summing up to a jury on one occasion he made the following pronouncement: "Nought, members of the jury," he said, "added to nought still equals nought. And it remains nought if you add a third or a fourth nought to it or, indeed, any number of noughts." You may think, members of the jury, that the learned Lord Chief Justice did not have to draw very deeply upon his profundity of thought to arrive at or express that conclusion. I am not a profound thinker, but I venture to suggest to you, members of the jury, that that pronouncement of the Lord Chief Justice is as applicable to the present case as no doubt it was to the case over which he was presiding. The Crown has called eight witnesses, and when I have dealt with the evidence of each of them I am going to suggest to you that the Crown's score in this match is minus one.

'Now his Lordship will tell you what the Crown has to score in order to justify a conviction, but it must certainly be more than nought. And, if at the end of the case you are satisfied that the Crown has not achieved a higher score than that, your duty will be to return a verdict of not guilty. Members of the jury, the prosecution has no right, and I certainly have no duty, to refer to the fact that my client has himself elected not to claim his privilege of giving evidence. I hope you will note what I said, members of the jury, and I venture to think his Lordship will confirm it – that the giving of evidence by an accused person is a privilege granted to him by Parliament a little over sixty years ago. He has a right to give evidence. He has no duty whatever to do so. Of course, where a strong case is made out against a man, it would be very foolish of him not to claim his privilege. And a jury might well doubt whether a man in his right mind could be so foolish. And in such a case you might well be driven to the conclusion that his reason for not giving evidence was not folly but fear or knowledge of guilt.

'But where no case is made out against a man, or such a flimsy one that it cannot stand on its own feet, he is entitled to say: "I ask the jury to say that I am not guilty without hearing a word from me." That would mean, members of the jury, that such a man could in later years say that the jury decided in his favour without his going into the witness-box. In other words, members of the jury, it would not just be a verdict of "not guilty" which he would have obtained – which, for all his audiences in later years could tell, might have been a lucky verdict – it would not just be a mere acquittal but an acquittal which he could properly say for the rest of his life was due to the jury finding that the Crown had no case or no sufficient case against him. No question of a lucky verdict in such circumstances. If you only hear one side and on that side's evidence find in favour of the other side, that is an overwhelming victory for the accused which is bound to weigh in his favour for the rest of his life. And, if the matter is of sufficient public interest, in history thereafter. My client is a public man, members of the jury, and I am going to ask you in due course to say "we find this man not guilty on the word of the prosecution alone." I suppose that evil tongues will always wag while human nature remains as it is, but will not such a verdict so obtained make it far less likely that they will be heard after this case? It will certainly make it much more dangerous for the owners of such tongues not to curb them.

'So, members of the jury, I refer without hesitation to the fact that my client has not gone into the witness-box. Some of you may think it would have been better if he had done so. I should not quarrel with such an opinion. But what I do submit to you is that, having regard to the prosecution's evidence, there is absolutely no need for him to do so. The prosecution has in my submission scored nought or less than nought. If this were a game of cricket it would, of course, be necessary for my client to go in to bat and score at least one to gain the victory. But this is not a game of cricket and the rules are different. Before the prosecution can claim a victory at your hands it has to make such a score as to convince you of the accused's guilt. As I said before, his Lordship may well tell you how much that score must be, but no one could dispute that it must be not less than one.

'Now, members of the jury, I shall go through the prosecution's batsmen with you and examine with you how they fared. I don't include Mr Stuart who, as my learned friend says, adds nothing to the evidence. You may have noticed that my learned friend abandoned several of them at the outset. That was, of course, consistent with the fair way in which he conducts all his cases. But was it simply out of fairness that he threw Colonel Brain and Mr Piper – if not to the wolves, at any rate on the dust-heap? Why were these gentlemen called to give evidence if it was not considered that they were necessary witnesses for the prosecution? Is not my learned friend's reticence on the subject of their evidence also consistent with a natural desire on his part that you should forget that they were ever included in the prosecution's team? If the prosecution had a sufficient case without them, why were they called? If fairness was the only reason for abandoning them, why were they not abandoned before play began, and their names given to the solicitors for the defence? You may think that they were called because the case for the prosecution rested on this proposition – that virtually all the onlookers saw that this car did not stop at the "halt" line. That without such unanimity of evidence the Crown's case would be insufficient.

'Any couple of people may think they have seen something but, when it comes to convicting a person on their evidence alone, a prosecutor might well feel that, in view of the danger of mistake, it would be unsafe to launch a prosecution on their evidence alone. But, of course, if there is a host of witnesses that is quite a different proposition. Everyone saw that the car didn't stop. Well, you can't call everyone, but eight is a pretty good number. And so the case was presented. Eight reliable unprejudiced witnesses, unknown to either party. And where are they now?

'I will deal with their evidence individually in a moment. But, first of all, I ask you to consider how it is that there was this wealth of testimony available to the police. The answer is quite simple, members of the jury. And I venture to suggest that some at least of you, if you had seen a motor-cyclist badly injured, perhaps killed, in a collision with a car which did not wait, might swiftly have assumed everything against the car driver. We now know from the police inquiries, the result of which the police superintendent very fairly gave in evidence, that the car driver's wife was gravely ill and needed immediate assistance. There was ample help available for the injured man. The accused reported the occurrence within a few days. But none of this was known, or could be known, to the onlookers. They had seen a badly-injured man and a hit-and-run driver. A person would not be human if he or she were not immediately and violently prejudiced against such a driver.

'It is a very small step from anger and prejudice to belief in a state of affairs which anger and prejudice dictate. Can't you imagine the scene, members of the jury? This sort of thing: "Did he stop at the 'halt' sign?" "He couldn't have, could he?" In no time both parties to the conversation are convinced that the driver did not stop and that they saw him fail to do so. They only have to discuss the matter with other bystanders to convince themselves and everyone else of the fact that the car did not stop. And when I say convince, I mean convince. Colonel Brain, for example, who in fact only came out of the Blue Goose because he heard a crash, became convinced that he had actually seen the car before the collision, and that it crossed the "halt" line without stopping. Yet, in fact, he saw nothing of the accident at all except the results. Yet I accept the honesty of Colonel Brain without question. He had no wish to deceive you, members of the jury, I am quite sure. And yet he calmly says he saw the accident when he was inside the Blue Goose at the time. Why? For the reason I have given you, the mass-indignation which affected everyone present when the car drove off leaving an injured motor-cyclist behind.

'But what of the others, members of the jury, who might have seen what happened before the accident? It may be that during the hearing of this case you have tried to test the accuracy of my contention that the normal person cannot seriously think of two things at the same time. For example if, as I am sure you are, you are listening to me now – you cannot consider what you are going to have for dinner tonight or how to fill in next week's football coupons.

'Try it for a moment. If you do, you will find that you miss some of what I say, if you try to consider either of the other matters. Conversely, if you really listen to me, you cannot possibly come to a conclusion as to whether Wolves will beat Arsenal. One man in a million has an abnormally made brain and can do this sort of thing. But none of the witnesses in this case is put forward as having this abnormal power. How, for example, could the charming Miss Gaye or Miss Wagstaffe or Miss Hardcastle have seen anything at all? She was fiddling with her brooches, wondering which George was going to appear. How could the unhappy Commander Parkhurst have seen anything? He was concentrating on his dead son – killed twelve years before by a sports car. And it was a sports car my client was driving. As for Mrs Benson, she was thinking about driving a car herself and it was only when the crash occurred that she really took notice. Mr Piper's evidence my learned friend agreed could be safely disregarded. But what sort of a case is it, members of the jury, when witness after witness is to be disregarded?

'Mr Berryman's evidence I agree with my learned friend requires more consideration. But, when you give it that consideration, I venture to suggest to you, members of the jury, that it comes to nothing at all. In his case we do not know what he was thinking, but he agrees that he was probably thinking of something. You will remember that at first he said that he did not stop until *after* the accident. Is that conceivable, if he really saw the two vehicles approaching each other? It could only have been someone who did see them approaching each other and who remembered stopping – frozen in his tracks at the thought of what was going to happen – who could have given this evidence. It was only when I pointed out to him the significance of not stopping that he said perhaps he did stop. But surely he must have remembered stopping if he really saw what he says? I suggest to you, members of the jury, that Mr Berryman saw nothing at all until the actual impact. Whether he was thinking about Queen Elizabeth or about his garden we don't know but, whatever his thoughts, they were not centred on the motor-cycle or car. And, unless they were, he couldn't have seen them.

'The position about Mr Salter is rather different. He is a schoolmaster, and I agree that he is a normal, responsible individual who was at the scene of the accident and who *could* have seen it and how it happened. I repeat *could* have seen. The question is "did he?" It may help you if I remind you of Mr Salter's evidence. He says that he saw the motorcyclist come round the corner. Now just suppose that the car had stopped at the "halt" line and had then started off until it had arrived a few feet from the point of impact. Until the motor-cyclist came round the corner he couldn't have seen the car wherever it was. Now Mr Salter said that the motor-cyclist might possibly have been able to avoid the accident by stopping. He also says that the motor-cyclist was going at a moderate speed. If the last statement is correct, why didn't he stop?

'No one wants a collision. Whether the car had stopped at the "halt" line or not, the motor-cyclist didn't want to run into it. Then why did he? In my submission the only answer to that question is that the motor-cyclist was coming too fast. Now, it is common ground that the car stopped only just beyond the point of impact. Why? If it had been going fast you'd have expected skid-marks – but there were none. The road was dry. I suggest to you that Mr Salter's evidence simply will not fit in with the known facts. Schoolmasters can be just as prejudiced as anyone else. So prejudiced was Mr Salter that, although at first he said at the Magistrates' Court that he couldn't say whether the motor-cyclist could have stopped or not, he subsequently said that he did all he could to avoid the accident. Of course, if he was flying round the corner I dare say he did all he could, as there was nothing effective he could do. But if he was only going at a moderate speed how can he have done all he could? He, at any rate, must be presumed to have had his eyes on the road. He must have seen the car. Then why hit it? The only answer is because his speed was such that he couldn't avoid doing so.

'Now, members of the jury, I quite realize that the mere fact that the motor-cyclist was going too fast would be no excuse in this Court for the accused to have driven over the "halt" line. If he drove over the "halt" line without stopping he was plainly guilty of dangerous driving. But, if he did that, how was it he was able to pull up at once? It's not as though he'd been hit by another car even. It was a broadside-on collision with a light motor-cycle. That wouldn't slow down the car appreciably at all. Yet, within a foot or two, this car – which has charged across the "halt" line – is stationary. How does Mr Salter account for that? He can't. He simply says that he teaches history and is not an expert on statics and dynamics, but that he knows what he sees and he saw the car cross the "halt" line at a fast speed. If the car was going at a fast speed, and the motorcyclist only at a very moderate speed, you might have expected the car to pass harmlessly in front of the motor-cyclist. How does Mr Salter account for that? He doesn't. He simply sticks to his story.

'Possibly you may think that Mr Salter has been infected by the attitude of some of his more obstinate pupils who repeat the same old story, even though it has been completely disproved. But, whatever the reason for his attitude, I suggest to you that his evidence must be wrong. I hope, members of the jury, that, after the exhibition which Mr Salter gave in the witness-box, you may think I have done him more than justice in my submissions to you. I suggest that he saw nothing of the accident. He was wondering what cigarettes to buy, when there was a crash. D'you believe that Mr Salter saw anything more than the collision?

'I have now dealt with all the witnesses except one, Miss Anderson. She is the one witness who today says that the car stopped. Members of the jury, just as I have shown, I hope conclusively, that the story of the other witnesses cannot be the story of what they saw but only of what they subsequently believed they saw, so I will concede that Miss Anderson's evidence is no more reliable than theirs. But what I am entitled to say is that she does not exactly add to the strength of the prosecution.

'Now, members of the jury, I have dealt with all the witnesses. But, in coming to your decision, you will, I hope, bear in mind that the evidence of the witnesses is not the whole of the evidence. Witnesses may lie or be mistaken. But basic facts cannot. It is a basic fact that there was a collision. It is a basic fact that the accused's car stopped within a couple of feet of that collision. It is a basic fact that the distance from the "halt" line to the point of impact is rather less than that from the bend round which the motor-cyclist came. When you bear these matters in mind, members of the jury, I submit to you that the whole of the case for the prosecution has crumbled to nothing and that this is not a case where there is a doubt as to the accused's guilt, but that there is no doubt as to his innocence.'

Chapter Nineteen

The Summing-up

As the judge began his summing-up the heads of the jury turned towards him as though at the order of a drill sergeant.

'Members of the jury,' he said, 'the number of people killed every year upon the roads is in the region of 6,000, the number injured runs into six figures. The object of the laws against dangerous driving, and the object of Parliament in providing severe penalties for breaches of those laws, is to bring to an end the carnage and mangling which daily takes place. Having regard, however, to the figures to which I have referred, one can only conclude that Parliament has been singularly unlucky in its attempts to achieve its laudable objects, or that it has gone the wrong way about achieving those objects. It may be that other means should be adopted instead. One of my learned brethren has suggested that a motorist, who has an accident or is convicted of a driving offence, should be compelled to carry a plainly visible sign or signs to indicate the number of his accidents or convictions, at any rate for a period of years, until, by his careful and considerate driving, he is adjudged to have atoned for the past. But whether or not you think it would be a good idea to adopt such a suggestion, whether or not you think that there are other means which should be tried to reduce accidents, whether you are a pedestrian or a motorist, or both, it is your duty to disregard entirely all such general considerations.

'Your sole task is to say whether it has been proved to your satisfaction that the law has been broken in this particular case. No amount of sympathy for a man with an ill wife, or for a man of good character who is in public life, should deflect you in the least degree from finding him guilty of the offence charged against him if you are satisfied that he is guilty. Conversely, no prejudice against motorists, no desire to improve conditions on the roads, no fear that an acquittal may encourage bad driving should lead you to convict the accused if you are not satisfied of his guilt. You have to consider this one accident only, and to decide whether it was caused by dangerous driving on the part of the accused. The consequences of conviction or acquittal are wholly irrelevant, and you will be breaking the oath you have taken if you pay any regard to them.

'Now, to establish the charge in this case, the prosecution has to prove that the accused drove dangerously. In some cases it is necessary for a judge to explain in some detail what is meant by dangerous driving because, in a sense, any driving which results in an accident is dangerous. In this case a man was badly hurt, so that you might say there must have been danger as there was actual injury. And you might go on to ask yourselves where the danger came from, and to answer that question by saying that it came, at least partly, from the driver of the car. You may well think that it is a pity that Parliament has chosen to use this word which, in its ordinary meaning, does not necessarily imply fault on the part of anyone. The Courts have, however, of necessity enlarged the meaning of the word for the purposes of this offence and, before you can convict of this offence, you have to be satisfied that the driving was of a reckless or deliberately wrong character or at the least there was some fault on the part of the defendant.

'In the present case, however, you are relieved, in my view, from a detailed consideration of the necessary ingredients of the offence because it is conceded by the defence, and I think rightly, that, if the accused drove over the "halt" line without stopping, he was plainly guilty of dangerous driving. Conversely, it is conceded by the prosecution, again in my view rightly, that if you are not satisfied that the accused failed to stop at the "halt" line the charge has not been made out. So, members of the jury, all you have to do in this case is to consider whether you are sure that the accused did not stop at the "halt" line.

'Now, what do I mean by "sure". You cannot be completely sure, because to be as sure as that you would have had to be present at the scene of the accident and you would have had to be watching the car yourselves. In that case you would, of course, have been witnesses and could not be jurors. Consequently, you can only be sure by reason of what other people, the witnesses called in the case, have told you. Now, if you knew the witnesses personally, knew that they were careful, reliable people or, on the contrary, thoroughly unreliable, you could not try the case and it would have been your duty to inform me of the fact as soon as you were aware of it. So you have to decide the case on the word of people you've never to your knowledge seen before in your life. You see them in the witness-box for, it may be, half an hour or so – or it may be several hours. In any event you don't see them long enough to make a sure assessment of their characters. You must know people quite well before you can do that. So what are you to do? I suggest to you that you do this. If this had been a case where there could have been no question of a mistake, I would have suggested to you that, in order to be sure of the accused's guilt, you should – when all the evidence had been concluded – have been as sure of his guilt as if a trusted reliable friend of your own had told you that he had plainly seen the crime committed by the accused. Then you would be sure of his guilt. Similarly, in a case where a mistake could have been made, even by a trustworthy reliable witness, you must be as sure that no mistake had been made as if you had been told so by someone who you knew would not tell you a thing for certain if he or she might be mistaken.

'If, for example, a friend of yours with good eyesight and hearing said to you: "I was outside the Blue Goose and I saw the accused's car coming towards the 'halt' line. I was looking at it because it looked like the car of a friend of mine. I was expecting it to slow down and halt when, to my surprise, it came straight on and it only stopped after a motorcyclist had run into it," members of the jury, one reliable witness who said that would be worth ten or twenty witnesses of the kind you have seen. That is not a criticism of those witnesses. You cannot have a witness of the type I have mentioned, because I predicated that he or she should be well known to you. Such a person you would be sure had not invented such a story or made a mistake about it. So, in this case, you have got to be as sure as that, no surer but no less sure than if one reliable friend of yours had told you that he had plainly seen the thing for himself. And you will notice that, in the example I gave, your friend had a particular reason for watching the movements of the car. He had thought it might contain a friend of his. Even in such a case you could not be absolutely certain your friend was right. But, as I have told you, you cannot have absolute certainty in these matters. You have to have the next best thing. Call it a moral certainty, if you like.

'Here is another example. None of you know me. You only know that I am the judge presiding at this trial. Now, if I had said to you at the beginning of this trial, "I am sorry I am late, but the omnibus in which I was travelling had an accident," I hope you would feel that that was true. I might be making a false excuse. But I hope you would feel it was a moral certainty that it was true. Applying these tests, are you sure that the accused did not stop at the "halt" line?

'Now, in order to help you to arrive at a conclusion, I propose to review the evidence. But one thing I must say at the outset. You may think it a pity that the person who was actually driving the car, the accused, has not gone into the witness-box to tell you his account of the matter. He, you may say to yourselves, is the one person who knows whether he halted or not. But, even that isn't quite right, members of the jury, because just as counsel for the defence suggests that the witnesses for the prosecution were prejudiced against the accused, so might the accused be prejudiced in his own favour. Just as *they* might say – honestly but mistakenly – that he did not stop, so *he* might say – honestly but mistakenly – that he did stop, when he didn't. Moreover it is, of course, possible that he would deliberately tell you that he stopped when in fact he didn't. And it would be easy enough for him to say that if he were so minded. So that, members of the jury, even if the accused had given evidence it might by no means follow that your task would have been made easier.

'But something I must tell you, members of the jury. Counsel for the defence is entirely right when he says that an accused person has no duty to give evidence. It is a privilege of which he can take advantage if he wishes. You are certainly entitled to take into consideration the fact that he has not given evidence, but you may not find it very valuable to speculate as to the reason for his decision. Is it because he feared a similar cross-examination to that administered by his own counsel to some of the witnesses? Had he some secret – nothing to do with the case – which he was afraid he might be compelled to disclose? Is there some other reason? I do not know nor can you.

'But you are entitled to say this to yourselves. If the case had been of a different kind, theft or fraud or something of that kind, then the absence from the witness-box of the accused you might think very strange indeed. Again, if the evidence in this case had been more compelling, you might think his absence strange. It is true that, even if you consider the evidence weak, he takes a risk by not giving his own evidence and submitting himself to cross-examination, but you are entitled to consider his counsel's submission that the case is so weak that in effect it calls for no answer. And in years to come it will be an advantage to the accused, says Mr Olliphant, if he can say he was acquitted without having to give evidence himself. Be that as it may, members of the jury, I propose to say no more about that aspect of the case. Cases have to be decided upon the evidence called before the jury, and it is upon that evidence that you will either convict or acquit the accused.'

The judge then proceeded to deal in detail with the evidence of the various witnesses. When he had dealt with them he went on:

'That is the whole of the case, members of the jury. Remember that it is not for the accused to prove that he did stop at the "halt" line, but for the prosecution to prove that he did not. Once again and for the last time I ask you this question: "Are you sure that he did not?" Your answer to that question will enable you to decide upon your verdict, and this I now ask you to do.'

Chapter Twenty

The Truth

Half an hour later the jury returned to Court.

'Are you agreed upon your verdict?' asked the clerk.

'We are,' said the foreman.

'Do you find the accused Michael Barnes "guilty" or "not guilty"?'

'Not guilty.'

'Not guilty, and that is the verdict of you all?'

'Yes.'

'You are discharged,' said the judge to Michael.

Ten minutes later he and Andrew were smuggled out of a side door into a taxi.

'Where shall we celebrate?' asked Andrew.

'At the hospital,' said Michael.

'Are you going to tell her?' said Andrew.

'I can now,' said Michael. 'They've managed to keep the papers away from her, but she's so much better that I feel I can tell her. I'm bursting to. And she's bound to learn about it anyway from other people in two or three weeks. I think we'll take in a bottle. I'll tell the driver to stop somewhere.'

He did so, and shortly afterwards they bought a bottle of champagne. When they were back in the taxi Andrew said:

'You were damned lucky.'

'I know.'

'But I give you full marks. There are not many people who would have stopped at perjury as you did.'

'Perjury? What d'you mean?' said Michael. 'Don't you believe my story?'

'No,' said Andrew, 'I don't.'

'Good God!' said Michael, 'and you've stood by me all this time thinking me to be a liar.'

'Not all the time. I did believe you at first. Anyway, one doesn't drop a friend because one thinks he's a liar.'

'But I'm amazed,' said Michael. 'You really think the car didn't stop at the "halt" line?'

'Not at all,' said Andrew. 'I'm as sure that it stopped as you are.'

'Then ...' started Michael, looking very astonished, but he didn't finish.

'You're an odd fellow, Michael,' said Andrew. 'You wouldn't commit perjury to save yourself, although you knew it was a grave risk not to, and yet you sit here and lie to me, an old friend, like a trooper.'

'Lie to you – how?' asked Michael.

'That's a lie in itself, and you very well know it,' said Andrew. 'Take that innocent, surprised look off your face and ask me why I'm sure the car stopped at the "halt" line.'

'Well – why?'

'Because I know Sheila almost as well as you. And I'm sure *she* wouldn't tell a lie. You weren't in the car, old boy. It was Sheila who had the accident and she told you she'd stopped.'

'How on earth did you know?' asked Michael.

'Well, of course, I couldn't and didn't until you refused to give evidence. At first, naturally, I thought your refusal was because you hadn't stopped – but you assured me that you had, and I believed you. Suddenly I thought of the only explanation that would fit. And that was it.'

'Well, you're quite right,' said Michael. 'She came back in a terrible state. She ought never to have been allowed to go out by herself. She panicked after the accident, and rushed home to me. She was desperately ill but she was able to tell me her story. And I believed her. I whisked her off to hospital. Then I came to you. Thank God for Olliphant. He understands independent witnesses.'

'But not as well as we do now, old boy,' said Andrew. 'He was pretty good but we could have bowled them out much quicker. They all said you were driving the car. That's because *you* gave yourself up and *you* were in the dock. It would have shaken all those good people who saw everything so plainly and so certainly if they knew that you weren't even in the car.'

'D'you think Olliphant guessed?'

'Not for a moment. He must have thought you were lying about stopping.'

'But he still went on with the case.'

'He had to. A barrister can't throw up a case just because he *thinks* his client is lying. He must *know* it. And he couldn't. After all, I didn't *know* it. I just knew it.'